Frantic Flight

Angela Dorsey

Frantic Flight

Cover and inside illustrations: Jennifer Bell
Cover layout: Stabenfeldt A/S
Copyright: Text © 2005 by Angela Dorsey
Typeset by Roberta Melzl
Edited by Bobbie Chase
Printed in Germany 2005

ISBN: 1-933343-07-9

Stabenfeldt, Inc.
457 North Main Street
Danbury, CT 06811
www.pony.us

"She'll be home in fifteen minutes. You can take both her and the boy then." The woman glanced at the dirty five-year-old boy crouching in the corner of the shabby room. He watched them with desperate eyes, like a frightened animal that has nowhere to run. A satisfied expression swept onto her face. Finally she would be rid of the two orphans her husband had forced upon her.

"She better be a good worker. Her scrawny little brother won't be very useful," the man said with a brutish voice. "He'll be more of a burden than anything."

The woman turned sharply toward him. "But if you want her, you have to take him, understand? That was our deal." She thumped her teacup down on the table to emphasize her words and the last drops in the cup splattered onto the hard surface.

"Mama?" A timid voice came from the doorway to the bedrooms. She turned in her chair and immediately her face softened. "What is it, Serena?"

The well-dressed, dark girl came forward warily. She paused before speaking, as if taking time to gather her courage. "Please don't do this, Mama. It's not right. You know it's not right. Giselle's had such a hard life. She needs us."

The woman held her arms out. "Come here, my love. There's nothing to worry about." Her arms encircled her daughter. "This is a wonderful opportunity for Giselle. Her new family will send her to school. You don't want to stop her from getting an education, do you? And the boy will go to school too."

"But Mama..."

"Now you listen to me, young lady," the woman interrupted with a hard voice. She pushed Serena back so she could look into her eyes. "Giselle will be better off in the city."

Serena wasn't able to hold her mother's gaze and her eyes dropped to the ground. The despair and frustration on her face said what she didn't dare speak aloud – that she didn't believe her mother's words.

The woman's tone lightened. "Once she learns to read and write, she can write to you. You'd like that, wouldn't you, darling?"

A whimper came from the corner. The little boy was crying again. The woman glanced at him with disgust, and then fought to compose her features before looking back into Serena's worried face. "Now go get changed out of your school clothes. You should have done it hours ago."

The girl lowered her head and turned toward the doorway. Reluctantly, she shuffled a few steps, and then suddenly spun back around. Words flew from her mouth. "But I've heard people aren't nice to the restavecs sometimes, Mama. And they don't let them go to school even when they say they will. They're not given enough to eat and they have to sleep on the floor with rags for blankets. They're made to work all the time, and..."

Serena's mother raised her hand. The girl's mouth snapped shut and she stepped away in a single fluid motion. She knew from experience that her mother's slaps were not gentle.

The woman slowly lowered her hand. "You heard wrong, Serena. That's what I get for letting you hang around the school-house too much. That teacher of yours is spreading lies. From now on, you come home straight after school. With Giselle gone, there's going to be more work around here for you to do anyway."

The girl tried one more time, her voice a wheedling whine. "But Mama..."

"That's enough, Serena! Go! Now!" The woman's words bit through the air, her patience completely gone.

Serena turned and looked at the boy cowering in the corner. Tears brimmed in her eyes. "Good-bye, Robert," she whispered. "I wish..." Unable to say more, she fled from the room.

The woman sighed and lifted her bulk from the chair. She grabbed the cracked teapot from the counter.

"A strong looking girl," the man said behind her. "She'd make a good restavec."

The woman spun around, her eyes full of fire. "That one is my daughter," she spat at the man. "She will never be a servant!"

6

"The other isn't your daughter?" asked the man. He ran his fingers through his dark, oily hair.

"No. She is nothing to me," said the woman as she sat down, the teapot handle clenched in her fist. She tipped the spout toward the man's empty cup. "Would you like some more tea?" she asked, her voice sweet once again.

Giselle was so tired. Gratefully, she looked up at the mountain looming in front of her. The sun had almost disappeared behind it. Time to go home.

With a groan, she pushed herself up from the row of vegetables she'd been weeding. She stretched to ease the clenched muscles in her back, her face squinting in pain. She'd been hunched over the greenery for far too long, ever since early that afternoon when Madame Celeste had told her, in no uncertain terms, that she wanted the entire garden weeded by nightfall. And that was after Giselle had scrubbed all the floors in Madame's house and washed the dirty dishes Giselle was sure Madame Celeste had saved for the last week.

Giselle had worked extra hard to do everything Madame had asked. She'd even labored through the oppressive heat in the hottest part of the afternoon, when everyone else in their tiny Haitian town found a shady spot to rest. Giselle couldn't have Madame getting angry with her to-day, because today she had to collect the wages she'd earned over the last month. Her aunt had told her that morning that she expected to see everything Madame owed her that night when she got home.

Giselle walked to the door of the small mud house. Madame wasn't a rich woman. The only way she could afford hired help was because of the income she received from selling the vegetables from her garden and occasionally renting out her pony, Domi. Even then, she couldn't afford to hire anyone other than Giselle, thanks to the incredibly low sum Giselle's aunt charged for her niece's labor.

Giselle knocked on the door. There was no response. She waited a moment, and knocked again, a little louder. When there was no obvious sound from within, Giselle held her ear next to the flimsy door. Maybe Madame was asleep.

Even if she's sleeping, I have to wake her, thought Giselle. And she's tried to pretend she was asleep before, to get out of paying. She's probably hoping I'll go away. She sighed. She couldn't force Madame to pay her, and Aunty was going to be furious with her if she didn't get at least some of the money owed her.

"Madame Celeste!" The door shook as she pounded on it with her fist. "Madame, please. I must speak with you," yelled Giselle. "I can't go home until I speak with you," she added, so that Madame would think she would wait all night if she had to.

Giselle heard the metallic scrape as the bolt was pulled back, and then the door opened a crack. "Be quiet, girl. Are you trying to disturb all the neighbors?" said a reedy voice.

"I'm sorry, Madame," replied Giselle politely. "But Aunty told me I must get my wages from you tonight."

Madame answered her but the words were so low that Giselle couldn't understand what she was saying.

"I'm sorry, Madame. I can't hear you." She turned her head to hear better.

"I said I won't have your money until tomorrow. Are you deaf?"

"But I must have it tonight," Giselle said. She hated to hear the panic rising in her voice, the pathetic desperation. But what would Aunty do if she turned up empty-handed?

Ever since Giselle's uncle, her mother's brother, left to work in the sugar plantations across the border, Aunty had been cruel to Giselle and Robert, her little brother. Giselle had known that her aunt felt she had enough mouths to feed with her own children, and that the two orphans were an inconvenience to her, and so she never minded working and giving all her money to her aunt. She felt that at least she should pay for Robert's and her food. In her ignorance, she thought that would be enough to make her aunt feel more kindly toward them. It didn't.

One week after their uncle left, their aunt told Giselle that she wished both Giselle and Robert had died of the fever that killed their mother and father. Giselle was aghast. Though she'd known they were a burden to their aunt, she hadn't realized how much their aunt disliked them.

In the weeks that followed, their aunt became even more abusive. Only Giselle and Robert's two cousins, Serena and Pierre, knew of their mother's seething anger, and both of them tried to appease her in their own way. When they realized there was no saving Giselle and Robert from their mother's rage, Serena started spending a lot more time at the school and Pierre left with his friends as much as possible. Giselle's aunt blamed her and Robert for her children's absence.

9

"I tell you, I'll give it to you tomorrow. Are you stupid?" hissed Madame Celeste, bringing Giselle's thoughts back to the present. "Monsieur Dupont comes tomorrow for the pony, and then I can pay ."

For a moment, Giselle couldn't speak. Could hardly breathe. When she finally was able to form words, her voice felt scratchy. "Monsieur Dupont? He's coming for Domi?"

"Yes," said the woman, then her voice became softer. "I know you like this pony, but he is getting old, Giselle. When I have enough money, I'll buy a younger pony to take his place. You will like this new one just as much, oui?"

"But Madame," emotion choked Giselle's voice. "Monsieur Dupont buys horses and ponies for slaughter."

"Yes, but that is the way of life, Giselle."

"But Madame..."

"No more talking. Come back tomorrow and I'll give you your money." The door shut in Giselle's face. She stood for a moment, breathing heavily. Tears sprang from her eyes. She had to do something, but what? If only she had the money to buy Domi, but the wages Madame owed her wouldn't be enough to buy even one small black hoof.

A soft whinny came from across the yard and Giselle's shoulders tensed even more. She put her hands to her eyes and a sob broke the silence in the yard. "What can I do?" she whispered in a rough murmur. "I have to stop her somehow. She can't sell Domi to be slaughtered."

Giselle stumbled toward the pony's canvas shelter. As usual, the night had dropped over the town almost as fast as a blanket falling from the sky. Halfway to Domi's shack, she realized she hadn't watered the pony since late afternoon and groped for the water pump. As the bucket filled with water, she used the time to compose herself. There was no point in worrying Domi. And maybe, if she could just think, she could come up with a plan. When the bucket was full, she carried it to Domi's shelter and stepped inside. The pony greeted her with a nicker.

"We have until tomorrow, Domi. I'll think of something," Giselle whispered and put the bucket at the pony's hooves. "Maybe if I promise to work for free for the next three or four years, Madame will keep you. She'll recognize it's a good deal for her. She's not unreasonable."

But Aunty is, Giselle suddenly realized. And she won't like it if I don't bring money home even from one job. Or she might find out that I'm buying Domi with my labor and try to sell him to the knacker herself. I'll have to swear Madame Celeste to secrecy.

Giselle gently rubbed the gray pony's withers as he took a long drink. Madame was right about one thing. Domi was getting old. He was thinner than he used to be and his hair didn't have the same sheen it once had. He needed her to take good care of him.

"Don't you worry, Domi. I'll figure it out and stop by first thing in the morning to talk to Madame," she said softly. Her fingers traced down the center of where she guessed the white streak on his face would be if it weren't too dark to see. "And I'll figure out what to do with Aunty too," she continued. "Maybe I can take another job or ask for a raise at one of the other places I work. As long as Aunty doesn't find out, we'll be okay."

The pony nuzzled her arm. Giselle drew a trembling breath and gave Domi a quick hug around the neck. "Goodnight, my friend,' she whispered and left the shelter. His soft whinny followed her into the night.

Giselle passed through the back streets like a shadow. She knew it was dangerous to wander around the unlit streets after night fell. Unsavory characters seemed to come out of nowhere when the sun went down, even in her small town.

In the distance, she heard the voodoo drums begin their steady beat. They would continue until dawn, she knew, as they did almost every night. Giselle hurried into her aunt's back yard and closed the metal gate behind her.

A sudden chill ran down her back and she froze. Someone was watching her. She could feel it. She strained her eyes trying to pierce the cloak of darkness. And she saw something! A man! Or half a man? A split second later she knew what she was seeing – Pierre's clothes, drying on the clothes line. She almost laughed out loud.

Then she heard a slight movement in the shadows beside her. Her heartbeat swelled to thunder in her ears and the hair on her arms prickled in abrupt fear. So it hadn't been her imagination! Someone was there, in the darkness, watching her.

"Giselle?" The voice was as soft as a breeze.

Giselle felt an explosion of relief. It was only her cousin, Serena. "Yes, its me," she whispered.

A warm hand touched her arm. "Come, quick. Behind the mango tree. And quietly. She can't know you're here."

"What is it? What's wrong?" Giselle asked as she stepped behind the sturdy tree trunk.

Serena released her arm. "Giselle, you must go. You must run away. Tonight." She shoved a sack into Giselle's hands.

Giselle pushed the sack back at Serena but her cousin wouldn't take it. "What? Why? Why must I leave? I don't understand." She couldn't stop her voice from breaking. Did Serena hate her too now?

There was a long silence from Serena. Giselle searched the intense darkness for her cousin's face. If she could just see one feature, maybe she could comprehend why Serena was acting so strangely. "I don't understand," Giselle finally added. "I thought we were friends. I thought…" She couldn't finish.

Serena's response was to throw her arms around Giselle. She laid her head on Giselle's shoulder and sobbed quietly. "What is it?" Giselle asked again, almost overwhelmed with relief. Serena still liked her. She patted her cousin on the shoulder. "Please, tell me."

"You must go," choked Serena. "Mama has..." She stopped. In the distance, the voodoo drums became louder.

"Has what?" asked Giselle, though she didn't want to ask. Didn't want to hear the answer.

Serena pulled away and Giselle waited fearfully as her cousin gathered her emotions. When Serena spoke, her voice was forced, strained. "She is sending you away, to be a...a restavec."

Giselle staggered backward, and only Serena's hand on her arm kept her from falling. Now that Serena had started, she couldn't stop. "She and an agent are waiting in the house for you to come home," she continued quietly but insistently. "That is why she asked that you get your money from Madame Celeste tonight. She is planning to take your wages from you before you go. And Giselle, there is more."

"What?" The word seemed to come from somewhere outside Giselle. She leaned against the tree, her knees shaking.

"Robert is to go as well."

The thought of her baby brother being taken to the city to work as a restavec, a child laborer, was even worse than being taken herself. Giselle knew she could survive something like that because she would remember what it was like not to be a restavec. Restavecs were usually only kept while they were children and young teenagers, and within a few years she would be turned out of her master's house to fend for herself. Somehow she would be able to survive. But Robert was only five years old. If he were taken now, he would grow up never knowing what it was like to have a family. His mind would be stunted and warped by the life he would lead as a restavec.

"The police," choked Giselle. But even as she said it, she knew there was nothing they could do. Robert would be taken toward the city early in the morning, long before the police station opened for the day. Even if she could find an officer that night, it would be too late. The agent would shortly take Robert from her aunt's house and hide him away until morning. And perhaps worst of all, she knew it was unlikely a policeman would believe her. All her aunt needed to say was that Giselle was lying or crazy or stupid, and Giselle knew how convincing her aunt could sound, how sweet and caring, when she wanted to. "What am I to do, Serena? How can I save him?" she whispered, her voice desperate.

"You can't. It's too late for him. But it's not too late for you, Giselle." She reached down and felt the ground for the cloth bag. Giselle hadn't even realized she'd dropped it. Serena pushed the bag of food back into Giselle's hands. "Run away, Giselle. Into the mountains. To some other town. Just get away from here. You can't let this man take you."

"But Robert..." A high-pitched whine.

"No buts," said Serena, sounding uncannily like her mother. "You can save yourself. Now go, before it's too late. They'll come looking soon, and then we'll both be caught."

Giselle stumbled toward the gate. The dirt beneath her bare feet felt strangely cold, the bag in her hands, insubstantial. Her life had just reached a new low, something she hadn't thought possible. Before tonight, she may not have had parents or an education, she may have been punished by her aunt for every little thing, but at least she had a home to go to. At least she and Robert had a family. But no more. It was all over. She'd finally lost everything. Everything but her freedom – and that would be stolen from her too, if she didn't act quickly. Serena was right. Her only hope was to leave. If she stayed anywhere near the town, her aunt and the agent would find her. She had one chance, and that was to run and run far, somewhere her aunt wouldn't think to look.

She turned at the gate to find Serena behind her and pulled her cousin into one last hug. "Thank you for warning me. And for the food. You risked yourself for me. If your mother finds out..."

"You are like my sister, Giselle," Serena whispered. "I had to warn you. And don't worry, Mama doesn't treat me as she treats you."

14

"I am going to miss you." Giselle cried softly as she pulled away from her cousin.

"I'll miss you too," Serena said. Giselle could tell she was trying to stay strong, trying not to cry. To make it easier for me to go, she realized, and fresh gratitude for her cousin welled up in her heart.

"Good-bye. My sister," Giselle murmured and opened the gate. She heard Serena's muffled sob behind her, but didn't look back.

Her bare feet whispered over the ground as she ran down the dark alley. At the end of the narrow street she stopped and leaned against a cement wall. "Oh, Robert," she gasped. For a single moment she considered going back.

Maybe Aunty will listen if I beg her. Maybe she'll relent if I promise to work harder or for longer hours. Or I can volunteer to go with the restavec agent as long as Aunty lets Robert stay.

Giselle shuddered. In her heart, she knew it was no use. Her aunt wouldn't listen to her. If she turned back, they would both be sent away.

"I'm sorry, Robert. Please, please, please forgive me." She choked back another sob, and then turned and melted into the night, the sound of her step smothered by frenzied drumbeats.

"Where is that girl? She's never been so late before," said the woman. She raised her sturdy body from the chair and walked to the front door.

"Aunty?" The boy's thin voice came from the corner. "I'm hungry."

The woman didn't look at him. She opened the door and leaned out into the night. Light spilled from the house and caught a movement in the yard. "Giselle! Get in here this instant. What are you doing, sneaking around the yard like that?"

The dark form shrunk back and the woman heard a gasp – Serena's gasp. "Serena?" she demanded. "Is that you?"

"Yes, Mama," Serena said as she stepped from the shadows, her shoulders hunched and eyes lowered.

"What are you doing out here?"

"Nothing."

"Look at me!"

Serena trembled as she looked up into her mother's eyes. She could only hold the iron gaze for a moment before looking away.

"You warned her!" the woman roared. She grabbed Serena by the arm and jerked her inside the house.

There was the scrape of a chair as the man jumped to his feet. "She better be coming home tonight, Madame, or our deal is over."

"She can't have gone far," the woman said, turning on him like a lioness. "Where is she supposed to go? Into the mountains? She'd know she'd never survive there. No, you'll find her on the streets, Monsieur, or visiting Madame Celeste's pony, three streets over." She pointed in the direction of Madame Celeste's house. "She has nowhere else to go."

The two glared at each other for a long moment, then the man growled and strode to the corner. He grabbed the boy by the arm and hoisted him to his feet. "If I don't find her, I'll be back. You can count on it."

The woman snorted with laughter as she stepped out of his way. "What kind of man are you if you can't catch a little girl? Go. Get out of my house!"

Any response the man might have made was drowned out by Robert's sudden screams. "Aunty! Aunty! I'm sorry! I'm sorry! Aunty, please!" he shrieked as the man dragged him out the door.

"Mama!" yelled Serena, her voice full of condemnation. "How can you do this?"

The woman didn't even hear her. With an expression of triumph on her face, she marched to the door and slammed it behind the man and boy, shutting Robert and Giselle out of her life forever.

Giselle ran headlong through the night. She didn't know where she was going. The only thing she knew was that she needed to put as much distance between herself and her aunt's house as possible.

She ran until her breath was coming in gasps and her legs felt rubbery and weak. Finally, she dropped to her knees beneath a tall palm tree at the edge of town. As she fought to catch her breath, she looked up at the mountains. She could barely make out their silhouettes in front of her, but the stars beaconed above them like little flares of hope. Could she go there to live? Could she survive there?

No, that's not the important question, she realized. Can I avoid the agent if I don't go into the mountains? That's what I really need to know, because if I can't, then I have no choice. I'll have to go, and worry about how to live once I'm there.

The problem was she didn't know anything about surviving in the wild Haitian mountains. She didn't know which plants were edible, which thorns were poisonous, which streams and pools contained water good enough to drink. The only thing she did know was that the thunder of voodoo drums rolled down from the foothills almost every night, and that poisonous snakes occasionally slithered from the unchecked undergrowth to be killed by the townspeople. She shuddered. Then there were the stories of tarantulas and toxic tree toads.

But still, none of what she'd heard was as terrible as the thought of leaving Robert behind. Tears spilled down her face. The idea of leaving him was like a death knell. Robert, her sad, skinny little brother, who she always thought would be beside her, whom she'd promised her mom and dad she'd always care for, was lost to her now. She thought of how he would snuggle up next to her every night and listen as she whispered stories of better times in his ears, of how he'd cuddle closer when she'd promise him she'd never leave him, never abandon him.

Only now she had.

She remembered saying good-bye to him that morning. He'd hugged her hard, just as he'd done every morning since their uncle left, and begged her not to go. As usual, Giselle had to pry his desperate arms from around her neck and promise him she'd see him that evening. Yet this morning he hadn't been comforted. She had to promise him twice more before his little arms finally released her, and even then she could tell he didn't want to let her go. Had he somehow known this morning would be their last morning together? Had he sensed something was about to happen? Or maybe he'd heard their aunt say something that he was too young to understand, but that still made him afraid?

Giselle's sobs abruptly ceased and she ground her teeth together. It wasn't fair! There had to be some way to help her little brother. She dashed away her tears, then held her hands in front of her eyes. She was strong for a twelve-year-old, she knew. Was she really helpless? Could desperation give her additional strength, and love for her brother lend her courage? Do I have more power to help Robert than I think I do?

"Of course not," she whispered. "I'm just a kid. What can I do?"

But the thoughts continued. They expect me to run and hide, probably nearby. Aunty might even expect me to come home, begging and crying, after the agent leaves. The only thing they won't expect me to do is to go back for Robert, to try to save him myself.

Giselle's heart raced as she climbed to her feet and looked back in the direction of her aunt's house. Yes, she was sure she was right. She had more power than they knew – she had the advantage of doing the unexpected. They thought she would act defensively and try to save herself, and they would react accordingly. They wouldn't expect her to go on the offensive, to go back to save her brother.

I promised Robert I'd never leave him. I told him I'd see him tonight – and I will, she vowed. Everyone Robert's ever loved has been stolen from him. Everyone but me. I won't leave him. Either we run away together, or not at all.

She squared her shoulders and started back toward her aunt's house. If the restavec agent caught her, then so be it – but she would not break her promise to her brother.

"Claude!" the man yelled when he drew near the shed, the boy's arm still clutched in his unrelenting grip.

A large shadow moved away from the door. There was the sound of a match being struck, and a tiny flame flared in the night. It brightened the ragged, pink scar jagging down Claude's cheek. The guard lit his cigarette and inhaled deeply, then held the match flame out toward the man and child to see them better. "Yeah, Boss?"

The man pushed the boy forward. "Put him with the others. I've got a runaway." The child fell against the wall of the shed, crumpled to the ground, and covered his head with his hands.

Claude appraised the child. "He's a scrawny one," he said, then flipped his wrist. The match went out.

"His sister's the one who's worth something. This one was thrown in for nothing."

"She worth hauling that skinny kid all the way to the city?" asked Claude. He raised his cigarette to his mouth again. The tip glowed red as he inhaled.

The man shrugged. "We'll see," he said. "Give me your machete, eh?" When Claude put the cold hilt in his hand, the man swung the giant knife, testing its weight.

"You know where to find her?"

"Yeah," answered the man as he moved off. Almost instantly, he was swallowed by the night. "I'll be back soon." The words floated back, disembodied and eerie.

Claude approached the child. "Come on, little man," he said, his voice gentle. "Big Claude's not going to hurt you. Just so long as you do what I say."

At the guard's feet, the boy began to weep quietly.

Giselle calculated her options as she crept back toward her aunt's house. If she was going to succeed in this wild venture, she needed a plan – and it had to be a good one. One of the first things she should do, she decided, was find a disguise. The agent would be looking for a tall girl with two pigtails, wearing a dirty, faded-to-almost-white, cotton dress. The way it was now, the lightness of her dress would be like a beacon in the night, drawing him to her. No other unescorted women or girls would be out after dark, and if he saw a lone figure in a pale dress, he'd know it was Giselle.

She needed to find some boy's clothes. The agent wouldn't be suspicious of a boy walking the dark streets. He'd assume the boy was coming home from working late in the fields or visiting friends. And she knew exactly where to find a t-shirt and some jeans – from the clothesline in her aunt's yard. Her cousin, Pierre, was only slightly bigger around than she was and, though he was taller, she could fold the pant legs up to the right length.

The rest of her plan fell quickly into place. First, she would stop at Domi's shelter and quietly steal him away. Then she would continue on to her aunt's house to take Pierre's clothes. Next, she'd mount the pony and the two of them would search for Robert. She felt bad taking Domi, but she needed him. With his speed and stamina, she was far more likely to find her little brother before the sun rose, and besides, she couldn't just abandon the pony to be taken away by Mr. Dupont the next morning. Last of all, she would free Robert while the agent was out looking for her, and the three of them would run away together and hide.

Giselle crept along the dark roads, watchful of any sound or movement. She heard the occasional voice, but they all came from the wider streets where the flickering streetlamps battled the night. The distant thunder of the drums swirled around her, making the shadowy streets seem even more ominous and foreboding. As she approached Madame Celeste's

21

house, she prepared herself mentally. She was feeling more and more guilty at the thought of stealing Domi.

If only Madame owed me more money, she thought. Then I wouldn't feel so bad. But we have to take him. Robert and I need him and he needs us. When I get older and get a job, I'll send Madame the money for him, even more than she'll get from Mr. Dupont. I swear it.

Her hand had just touched the gate leading to Madame's yard when Domi's small hoof struck the wooden frame of his canvas shelter. Instantly, Giselle froze. Someone was waiting there in the darkness for her, she was sure – and the pony didn't like whoever it was. She could feel his tension brushing against her, warning her away. His hoof hit the canvas wall again and he snorted.

Slowly, so slowly, Giselle retraced her steps and slipped into the neighbor's yard. Someone had been hiding near Domi's shelter waiting for her! And there was only one person it could be – the restavec agent. Her aunt must have told him Giselle would go to Domi. She swallowed nervously. It showed how well her aunt knew her habits if she'd sent the agent there.

A dog whined as she crept along the fence opposite the house. "Belle," she whispered, her voice as soft as breath. "It's okay. It's just me."

The dog, as black as night, padded toward her. Giselle held out her hand and the dog licked her fingers. "Good girl," she murmured and continued on her way through the yard.

Suddenly, the front door burst open. With a gasp, Giselle dropped to the ground. Light spilled through the open doorway and splashed across the yard.

"Belle!" The dog trotted toward the young boy who stood in the doorway. The boy knelt, put a pot on the ground, and rubbed the dog's hairy shoulders as she ate, murmuring words too low for Giselle to hear.

Giselle held as still as she could. She only hoped he wouldn't notice the lightness of her dress, stretched along the dark ground. Her stomach growled as she listened to the dog gulp down the scraps, despite her determination not to feel hungry. She hadn't eaten anything since lunchtime, and that had been only a single mango.

As soon as I get Robert, we'll eat some of the food Serena gave me, she thought. But only a little. Who knows how long it'll be until we find more?

The boy patted Belle one more time and then went back inside the house with the empty pot. The closed door shut in the light and Giselle

22

rose cautiously to her feet. Belle followed her to the front gate and Giselle stopped to scratch beneath the dog's chin before she closed the gate. "Thanks for keeping my secret, Belle," she whispered. "Have a good life."

She ran across the street and through another yard, then raced down another narrow unlit alley to approach her aunt's house from the back. The light was still on in the kitchen but, fortunately, both bedrooms were dark. The clothesline was at the back of the house and, unless her aunt was in her bedroom with the light off and looking out the window, Giselle could easily take the clothes she needed.

Bent double, she opened the gate and crept along the fence toward the clothesline. She noticed with relief that Pierre's clothes were still there. Since Giselle was the one who normally brought in the laundry, she guessed her aunt had forgotten the clothes were still hanging out. With shaking hands, she undid the clothespins holding one of his shirts to the line – and felt another momentary twinge of guilt. Pierre didn't have many nice clothes, and the shirt she was taking was his favorite. But it was the only dark-colored shirt on the line. She unpinned some pants, and with the clothes flung over her shoulder, hurried back the way she'd come.

Within seconds, she was racing down the dark alley away from the house. Half a block away, she threw her dress to the ground, turned the shirt inside out so the light colored emblem on the front wouldn't show, and slipped it over her head. Then she pulled on the jeans. Just as she'd thought, they were too long. She started to fold up the bottoms, but then stopped. She couldn't afford to have the pant legs unroll and trip her at a crucial time – like if she were running away from the agent. The material was too strong to rip with her hands. It wasn't until she took the jeans off and used her teeth to start the tear that she was able to rip the bottom of the pant legs away.

Trying to walk as boy-like as possible, she started down the alley. She'd done the easy stuff. Now she needed to find where Robert had been taken and rescue him. Then they could both go back for Domi. Maybe by then the agent would be tired of waiting for her to show up and be gone.

And once the three of them were together, the most overwhelming task of all would begin – she would have to build a new life for them. Somewhere. Somehow.

23

Domi. I am here. Weak and blinded for a time I am, but soon I will help you.

Yes, I will be silent. You say there is someone nearby who has malicious intent? Someone who wishes to do harm?

Oh, you say the one who waits in the night is not here to harm you. He waits outside, across the yard in the darkest shadows, for one who has already tried to come to you once tonight – your true friend, the girl who works for your person.

I am sorry, Domi. Yes, I understand the girl is your person and not this woman who professes to own you. The girl is the one who has claimed your heart. She must be kind to have won your love, dear Domi.

Do not worry. We will do our best to save her from this man who wishes her harm. But first we must find her, and to do that, we must get away without alerting the one who is watching and waiting for her.

My strength has returned. Come, I have an idea.

The man shrank back against the solid fence. Soft rustling noises were coming from inside the pony's shack. He knew it couldn't be the girl. There was only one entrance to the crude shelter, and he was watching it. The pony was probably just a little anxious, sensing he was waiting there in the darkness. He hoped its nervousness didn't warn the girl off.

The man scowled into the night as a new possibility presented itself. Maybe the girl had already come, sensed the pony's agitation, and guessed someone was there. If she had, he was wasting his time and, even worse, each moment she'd be getting farther away, making it harder to find and catch her.

But what if she hadn't come yet?

How much longer should he wait?

Giselle paused where the alley crossed another back street. Which way should she go? There were so many places the agent could be keeping Robert. All it would take was a single room in a single house and a house owner who didn't ask questions – something relatively easy to find in a town where most people struggled an unending battle with poverty. One little boy would be so easy to hide away.

A sudden thought leapt to Giselle's mind and she inhaled sharply. The agent wouldn't have come all this way just to get her and Robert. No, he would be gathering other children as well, either by convincing their poverty-stricken parents he was taking them to a life of opportunity in the city, or by taking the unloved ones, like Giselle and Robert. It made sense. The child labor agent would need to collect as many children as possible to make his trip to the city profitable.

And if he had a number of children with him, there were only a few places he could keep them locked away. No reputable establishment would rent to the agent, so that left a private citizen with an empty building large and strong enough to hold a few children. Giselle could think of five outbuildings that fit that general description right off the bat, with all of them being to the north. Without delay, she ran toward the nearest possible holding place, just three blocks away.

She was halfway there when the moon peeked over the mountain. It rose quickly, only a half moon, but its light was bright. Giselle changed her tactics and began dashing from this dark doorway to that unlit space between houses to a long shadow of a tree. She couldn't take a chance on being seen. Who knew how long the agent would wait at Madame Celeste's house? And he might have helpers. If he had a number of children, he'd need help managing them – which meant even as a boy, Giselle wasn't completely safe. An agent could grab a boy just as quickly as a girl to take to the city. Dressing in jeans and a t-shirt only kept her safe from instantly being recognized by the man who'd come for her and from strangers loitering in the night looking for trouble, not from additional agents.

When she saw the back of the building in front of her, she shot into the shadow of the wall and slowly, slowly, slid along the side. Her heart thundered in her ears and her fear made her breath too loud.

What if there's a guard outside the door? What if one of the agents hears me? What if he's standing just around the corner?

She reached the edge of the wall and stopped, too afraid to look around the corner at the door.

Robert is counting on me, she chided herself. I promised him I'd see him tonight. What am I? A coward? A weakling? All I need is to be strong for a second. Just long enough to peek around the corner. No one knows I'm here. I can do it. I have to do it.

Taking her courage in hand, she leaned to look around the corner. Moonlight splashed across the front of the shed. The door hung open. Giselle closed her eyes and shuddered. Unbidden relief flowed through her body. There was no guard.

But no children either. The building was empty.

She took a deep breath and, without wasting another moment, hurried on.

I'm sick of this waiting. There are still sounds from inside the shed. It could just be the pony, but maybe not. Maybe the girl slid beneath the canvas at the back. Maybe she's in there right now, laughing at me.

This cursed moonlight will make it even darker inside the shack. I'll need my flashlight.

Hey! It's not dark. The canvas has been cut away from the back of the shelter!

And what's that? A dog. A black dog, running out the back.

What? Is this black magic? How could the girl rip out the back wall without making a sound? Then communicate with the dog so it would make noise and keep me waiting here like a fool?

It's not possible. Is it?

Her aunt seemed awfully glad to get rid of her. There's got to be something wrong with her. Still, I made a good deal. I'm not going to let her go.

And there're people who'll pay extra for a girl like that. Maybe I can offer her to a circus. Depending on what she can do, she might be worth more than the others combined.

But first I have to catch her.

There was no one at the second place she tried, or the third. By the time she arrived at the fourth possible holding place, the moon had slipped behind a cloud, leaving Giselle to the mercy of the night. She stopped to still her breath before stealing toward the dark building. There was no guard at this one either, and Giselle crept to the door. It was locked. She knocked gently. There was no response. She tried again, a little louder, then whispered Robert's name. No response from inside the shed.

There was a slight noise behind her and Giselle spun around, every nerve instantly alert. A guttural snarl slid from the darkness. She threw herself back against the building as a white shape hurtled from the night. It came to a sudden, choking stop just a yard away from her. Outraged barking filled the air as the white dog backed a couple yards, and then ran at her again. This time Giselle heard the snap of the chain when it hit the end of its tether.

A shout came from inside the house and light poured from a small window, revealing the dog's sharp bared fangs and narrowed eyes. It lunged at her again, jaws snapping.

Within seconds, Giselle was racing down the street. The barking grew distant behind her – and then swiftly closer! The dog's owner had set it free!

Giselle ran faster than she'd ever run in her life, her fear lending incredible swiftness to her tired legs. She was too terrified to look back, but she knew the dog would gain on her quickly. And it was running silent now, which scared her even more. When she heard the thud of paws hitting the dirt road behind her, she somehow pushed herself to run even faster.

Then came a distant shout. The dog's owner! He was calling the dog home! Giselle didn't dare slow long enough to look back, but then she heard it bark again – farther away. It had broken off the pursuit!

Though her lungs were burning and she felt sick with fear, Giselle continued to run. At the end of the street, she finally stopped and looked back. There was no sign of the dog. She staggered toward a nearby fence and collapsed against it, holding her aching side and gasping for air. It was then she noticed that her food sack was gone. She must have dropped it in her panic.

I don't have time to feel sorry for myself, she thought desperately, and forced herself to stand upright. She looked up at the sky. The night was wearing down quickly. The moon was still covered with clouds, but she could see the cloud edge shining silver. Soon the moon would be free of its cover – and more than halfway across the sky. With a determined step, Giselle continued on.

Thank you, my dear Belle, for making noise in Domi's shelter. We needed to erase our tracks and get into position before the man realized we had gone. Now he will go to find the girl and we will follow. That way, if he catches her, we will be there to help her.

I know it is a risky plan, Domi, but we have no choice. Since we do not know where she has gone, this is the only way to be sure we can help her if he catches her.

There he is. His darkness moves from the hole in the back of your shelter. He stalks soundlessly down the alley. Now silently, silently, let us follow.

The last building she could think of was a fair distance away, on the farthest street to the north. Giselle had worked for the people who lived two houses down, and remembered the shed because it was painted a bright green and she'd thought it was pretty. Instead of taking the main street in front of the house, she slipped into the alley that lay behind. When the house and shed finally loomed out of the darkness, Giselle once again went into stealth mode. Quietly, she slipped along the wall and peered around the corner.

The second she saw the front of the building, she knew Robert wasn't there. Though it was late, the door was wide open and light spilled out to brighten pot of red flowers beside the door. Giselle slipped away from the wall and into the shadow of a mango tree standing in the yard, so she could see inside.

A melodious whistle floated from the doorway and a man sat on a bench just inside the door. He whistled as he carved an intricate design into a piece of wood.

Giselle leaned against the tree trunk, tipped her head back, and closed her eyes in an effort to control her tears. Her dad used to whistle that song, back in the days when he and her mom were still alive – when they were a family. They'd been so happy then, even though Giselle hadn't recognized it at the time. They didn't have much money and lived in a one-room shack, but they had enough to eat and a home of their own. And each other. They'd had each other.

In the evenings, her dad would sit in front of their tiny fire and tell her and Robert stories until they fell asleep. Her mom would either rub Giselle's back or play quietly with Robert. Back then, he was a contented toddler, always laughing and talking baby talk.

I'd give anything to have that back. To have them back, Giselle thought. I wish I'd known it was all going to end too soon. I'd have appreciated it more. I would've forced myself to stay awake to listen to all of Dad's stories, no matter how tired I was. But I thought I had years of stories left to listen to. I thought we would always…

She couldn't hold her sorrow back any longer. Tears gushed down her cheeks. It took all her willpower to not sob out loud. If only she could walk up to the whistling man and say her dad's name – and have him look up from his work and be her dad. A crazy, impossible dream but, just for a moment, she basked in the impossible happening. Her father would pull her into the circle of his arms and cry too, tears of joy. Giselle would hear her mom's gasp and look up to see her standing in the doorway behind them. Then her mom would rush forward to hug her, to stroke her hair, to say they would never be parted again. And all three of them would go to bring Robert home.

But this man isn't Dad. If he's married, his wife isn't Mom. There's only Robert and me left in our family. And whether we're ever going to be a family again or not is completely and totally up to me. No one else.

She couldn't afford to waste time on impossible fantasies, regardless of how sweet they were. She rubbed the heels of her hands against her eyelids trying to eradicate the tears, took a deep breath, and forced herself to turn away.

Yet, after taking a few shaky steps down the dark alley, she stopped and looked back. She couldn't see the man anymore because the angle of sight was wrong, but she saw the light spilling from the doorway. She heard his whistled song. For just one more moment, Giselle pretended that the strange man was her dad.

When she finally moved off, she felt as if part of her was left behind. Maybe a bit more of her innocence. Maybe more of her hope. The only thing she knew for sure was that walking away from that light-filled doorway was the most difficult thing she had ever done in her life. So far.

Giselle was two streets away from the whistling man, heading back the way she'd come so she could check the southern part of town, when she suddenly stopped. She'd just remembered another building, a ramshackle tin shack that sat in a grove near the fields where her cousin, Pierre, worked after school. Pierre had taken her and Serena there once to show them something he'd found there, something strange. He'd wondered aloud if a ritual might have taken place in the abandoned shed the night before and, even though it was daylight when they'd walked into the rusted interior, both Giselle and Serena were frightened by what they'd discovered – a strange scent in the air, a jittery energy that seemed to ooze from the walls. And a dark stain in the center of the dirt floor.

Serena suggested that red wine must have spilt there, but Giselle could hear the doubt in her voice. She too suspected the stain wasn't wine. The shack was stifling hot, despite being beneath the trees, and the heat pulled the odor from the earth. To Giselle, the air in the shack smelled of stale blood. They left shortly afterwards. It wasn't until they were blocks away that Giselle relaxed enough to ask Pierre who owned the building.

He'd shrugged. "No one knows," he answered. "That's why I had to check it out."

"I bet older teenagers hang out there sometimes," Serena suggested quietly.

Pierre shrugged again. "Maybe."

Giselle remained silent. She didn't want to say what she was really thinking – that some small creature had been killed in the shack, possibly sacrificed in some bizarre ceremony. She knew it was better for Serena to convince herself someone had spilled red wine. She wished she could do the same herself.

And it would be the perfect place to keep a bunch of children, Giselle realized. A chill swept through her body. The building is hidden away from prying eyes, yet it's not too far from town either. No one lives there, so the agents wouldn't have to pay anything to use it. There aren't any close neighbors to ask questions or to hear the children if they cry. She shuddered again. The thought of Robert in that horrible place made her feel sick.

Suddenly her hand flew to her mouth. What if she went there and instead of finding the children locked in the shack, she came across another ritual? The drums weren't coming from that direction, but that didn't mean something wasn't happening there, like a quieter ceremony, something far more sinister. But even as the possibilities flashed through her mind, she knew she'd have to check the building. Of all the places she could think of, the remote shack was the most logical for the agents to use. She couldn't just pretend it wasn't so.

She'd only retraced her steps a few yards when the feeling of being watched tingled down her spine. She could almost feel unfriendly eyes

35

glaring into the back of her head. The thought of the white dog leapt into her mind and she shrank back into the shadows. No white shape charged toward her. No growl or bark assaulted her ears.

It must be my imagination, she thought, and watched for another few seconds. Still nothing. So she mustered her courage and hurried toward the distant shack.

There's someone up ahead, walking toward me – a boy, I think. It's hard to tell in this darkness. I'll grab him when he comes by. He might've seen the girl or have some idea where she might hide.

But wait, he stopped. He's just standing there. Now he's running back the way he came. It doesn't make sense. I wish I could get a good look at him, but he's avoiding the light.

This boy is the first person I've seen on the street almost all night. I wonder what he's doing out so late? He's kind of small, so he can't be that old – certainly not old enough to be out wandering the streets alone. There's definitely something suspicious going on. Maybe he's a friend of the girl's and he hid her somewhere.

There's only one way I can know for sure. I'll follow him. Catch him. When I show him the machete, he'll talk.

Domi. I must go! Another needs me. Please, I know you are frightened but you must follow this man, watch him, and call me if he finds your girl. But be silent. Do not let him know you are here.

I will return soon. I promise.

Giselle willingly sacrificed stealth for speed. She could see no point wasting time being perfectly quiet until she came closer to the building, and if she ran she could cut down the minutes it would take to walk to the building from fifteen to ten. She paused only when she came again to the edge of the last wide street she had to cross. She'd avoided it last time by taking the alley. She glanced around again but could detect no movement. The only sound was distant drums. The town seemed fast asleep.

And there aren't any streetlights here, she reasoned. It's probably safe. Before stepping into the open, she looked up. The moon was almost free of its cloud cover. Any second, moonlight would spill across the earth. She had no time to waste. She raced into the street.

Halfway across, moonlight splashed around her. Two seconds later, she was across, safely engulfed in the shadow of a palm tree. Her heart rate eased as she looked back the way she'd come. Still nothing. She'd made it across unseen.

Giselle left the shelter of the tree and hurried into the nearby alley. It led directly to the narrow lane that would take her to her destination. Just a few more minutes and she might find her brother. And then the next impossible task would begin. She'd have to set him free.

There's the boy, running across that street, right through the moonlight.

Hey, that ain't no boy! It's her! Has to be – she runs just like a girl, light on her feet. Fast too. And isn't the hair in pigtails? She must've stolen some poor fellow's clothes.

I can't believe my good luck! She's heading out of town, right past where Claude is holding the kids. This might be fun. Won't she be surprised when I haul her back and throw her in with the others, then tell her she ran right into our arms? And she thinks she's so smart!

Maybe I'll finally get some sleep tonight. Claude hasn't done nothing but sit around all night. I bet he's even been sleeping. Not like me, chasing some brat all around town. And I'm getting tired. I'm glad this is almost over.

Giselle jogged down the narrow lane. Shrubs and trees crowded against the road, blocking out the moonlight, making it difficult to see. Suddenly she stepped into a deep pothole and went flying forward. Her arm whacked against a stone as she sprawled across the road, and for a few seconds Giselle rolled into a ball and squeezed her forearm to her body. Tears sprang from her eyes as she waited for the pain to subside. Finally, still gasping, she climbed to her feet and continued to run.

A few minutes later she crossed the rickety bridge, and then a little farther on she noticed a familiar break in the vegetation. She slowed to a soundless walk and turned onto the path leading from the road. The drums had been growing louder as the night wore on, and she was glad for once to hear the clamor increase. The noise would help to mask the subtle sounds of her approach, just in case someone was there to hear.

She crept into the scrubby forest that lined the footpath. She wasn't sure what she was going to do yet – if Robert was even there – but she knew it wasn't a good idea to approach the shack from the main trail. She said a quick heartfelt prayer that she would touch only tree trunks, branches, and leaves as she felt her way through the darkness, and not snakes or tarantulas. Something skittered in the bush to her right and she froze. A few seconds later, she heard small rustlings as the creature moved away from her. She exhaled in relief and continued on.

When she saw the break in the forest canopy ahead, she moved even more cautiously. The building was in the center of a small clearing, and Giselle crept to the edge of the trees, her heart pounding like mad. The shack was in front of her. Moonlight shone down on the rusty tin, illuminating the entire shed – and the man who leaned against the door. He was huge.

There was no doubt in Giselle's mind that she'd found her little brother at last. And this man was guarding him. His head drooped over his chest and he looked as though he might be asleep, but he was still a formidable foe. He could wake in an instant if he heard something, if he felt something. As if proving her reasoning, an ashy-faced owl hooted from the other side of the clearing and the man's head jerked up. Giselle watched breathlessly as he looked around the clearing, the whites of his eyes gleaming in the moonlight. Then the man stretched his arms above his head and relaxed again against the door. Giselle smiled in the darkness. The owl's cry had given her an idea.

She waited a full minute before she lobbed a stone to the far side of the clearing. The small rock bounced on the ground and the man jumped to his feet. He stalked in the direction the sound had come and peered into the forest. Then, with a muttered curse, he returned to the door. Two minutes later, Giselle threw another stone. This time the big man only looked up. The third and fourth times, he didn't even do that.

Moving stealthily, Giselle moved from her hiding place. She stayed close to the forest edge as she crept toward the back of the building. When her foot brushed against a cluster of leaves, she froze, her eyes locked on the guard. Her heart thundered in her ears as she waited. But he didn't look up. Her plan had worked. He was accustomed to the slight noises.

A few seconds later, she was at the side of the building and out of his line of sight, and then finally at the back. She felt along the metal wall. The trees grew close to the building at the back and the moonlight couldn't penetrate the tangle of leaves and branches. Giselle found a crack between two sheets of tin with her fingers and bent close to the ground.

"Hello. Is anyone there?" she said in the softest whisper.

There was no response.

"Hello? Robert? Can you hear me?"

There was a rustling noise from inside the shelter. Giselle waited impatiently for a response.

"Who are you?" came the frightened whisper of a young girl.

Come to me, Rocket. Please! Quickly! I am blind and weak, but I can open your stall door. You must come through the smoke. I know it is frightening. I know you can hardly see and can barely breathe. I understand that the thought of leaving your stall, where you have always felt safe, is terrifying – but you must come before it is too late. Your home is on fire!

Thank you for trusting me, my love. Now let me hold your mane. I am still too weak to walk unaided. Let us leave this place. Let us breathe the fresh night air. Come.

"My name is Giselle. Is there a little boy there? About five years old? He's my brother." Giselle's whispered words tumbled over each other in her excitement.

A sound of movement came from inside the shed, then, "He's here. He's sleeping."

Giselle closed her eyes and drew in a shaky breath. "Wake him up," she said, a little too loudly. She heard the girl's quick intake of breath. "Sorry," she whispered again. "Please wake him."

"What good will that do? He'll just start crying again."

Though she was anxious to talk to Robert, Giselle knew the girl was right. She needed to find a way to get him out first, then wake him and escape. The owl hooted again, almost over her head.

"Are you there, Giselle?" the girl's whisper came from the crack. She sounded desperate.

"Yes. How many of you are there?"

"Eight," came the hushed reply.

"Is there any other way out? Is there a window?" Giselle asked, her voice so soft she could hardly hear herself above the distant drums.

But the girl heard her. "No, only the door with the guard."

Giselle was puzzled. If there was no way out but the one door, why did the children need a guard to keep them in? Couldn't he just lock the door and go somewhere more comfortable to sleep? Unless...

"Is the door locked?" she asked, a hint of excitement in her voice.

"No, there's a rope tying it shut."

"Can you untie the rope?"

"No, but..." Movement from inside the shed. Low voices. Then the girl was back. "Mark has a knife. Just a little pocket knife, but it'll cut the rope."

"Okay," said Giselle. "Let me think for a minute." She unconsciously rubbed her bruised arm as she thought. There was just one guard and a rope between the eight children and freedom. If the guard could be distracted, somehow led away from the door, the children inside could cut the rope and scatter into the forest. But what could possibly lead the guard away from the door? Giselle inhaled sharply when the answer came. She leaned close to the crack in the tin. "I know what we need to do. But before I tell you, you have to promise me that you'll help my little brother escape. You can't leave him behind."

"I promise," the girl said, suppressed excitement making her whisper a little too loudly. She dropped her voice. "We all promise, anything you want."

"Okay," said Giselle. "Now listen carefully."

She left the road. I don't think she saw me behind her but still, for some reason she's heading toward the shed. Could I be wrong? Maybe she's not trying to run. Maybe she's looking for her brother. She's a cheeky one if she is. Thinking she can outsmart both me and Claude.

I need to handle this right. If I go into the clearing and start talking to Claude, she'll just hide in the bush and it could take us all night to find her. I need to stalk her, get closer to her, and take her by surprise. Hopefully, I can grab her before she even knows I'm here.

Hey, wait! Who's that?

When the children understood what they had to do, Giselle crept back into the trees. She knew they would need a few minutes to prepare themselves, to awaken the smallest children and caution them to be ready to run. When they were ready, they would move the plan into action. She waited breathlessly, almost unable to bear the suspense. This plan had to work.

"Hurry, hurry," one of the children inside the shed said in a loud whisper. Someone rattled the tin at the back of the shelter. The plan had been put into action.

"I can't fit," said another child, sounding panicky.

"I'll push you," said a third.

"What's going on back there?" the guard shouted. "You kids be quiet."

"Hurry, he's coming." More banging on the tin.

"I'm through," said Giselle, and she shook a bush at the back of the shed. It's branches scraped against the tin.

"My turn," said another child.

"Now mine." Banging. Scraping.

"Hurry! He'll be coming! Let me through!" Branches rustling.

"You kids can't fool me!" the man shouted. "I know you can't get out."

"Let's go!" Giselle yelled. She ran around the side of the building, heading back in the direction she'd come. "Hurry, hurry," she said in a differently pitched voice. Her feet whispered over the ground and she cried out when she reached the edge of the trees at the side of the shed, pretending a branch had poked her. "No! Go this way," she called out in a yet a different voice.

"Hey!" the guard yelled behind her. "You kids get back here!"

Knowing he'd finally been convinced, Giselle ran into the forest. She pushed at the branches and bushes as she ran, trying to sound like many people running through the undergrowth. She had to lead him far enough away to give the others time to cut the rope and run off. The man's heavy footfalls were lost in her noise, but she heard his voice, bellowing close behind as he charged into the trees. "You little brats! Get back here!" The plan was working perfectly so far. Now she just had to avoid being caught herself.

Suddenly, a tall, dark shape loomed out of the night directly in front of her, its arms spread out to catch her! Acting purely from instinct, Giselle dove to the earth and rolled between the man's legs, then was up and running again, hardly missing a stride.

"What the..." She heard the confused exclamation behind her. Then a loud "oof!" followed by angry shouts.

Giselle stopped short and looked back. It was too dark to see anything beneath the trees, but she didn't need to see to understand what was happening. The man who had been chasing her had run into another one who'd been sneaking toward the shed. Their angry voices shot toward her, and Giselle turned to run again. This was her chance to escape. What luck to have the two agents run into each other!

She couldn't help smiling as she moved, silently now, through the woods. By the time the two sorted themselves out, gave up on finding her, and went back to the shack, the other children would be safely away. The girl – Giselle wished she'd asked her name - would be taking Robert to the bridge Giselle had crossed earlier. Soon she would see her little brother. She had triumphed over the restavec agents!

She came to the narrow road and stepped out without looking. After all, the men were behind her, both of them. She was completely stunned when a dark shape detached itself from a nearby tree trunk. Moonlight flashed on corded muscles and the next thing Giselle knew, a hand clamped over her mouth.

"There you are," a rough voice said, and a man leaned over to peer into her face. Giselle tried to turn her head away from his putrid breath as he spoke, but his hand kept her immobile. He laughed. "Not so smart after all, are you?"

All she could do was shut her eyes.

The agent spun Giselle swiftly around, grabbed her sore right arm in an iron grip, and twisted it behind her back. Giselle would've cried out in pain if his other hand still wasn't over her mouth. She was completely helpless.

"We'll just wait here quiet-like, while Claude takes care of the cop," the man hissed in her ear.

The cop? Giselle blinked. Had she heard right? A policeman was here? Suddenly she remembered the confusion she'd heard in the second man's voice when she'd dived between his legs. Was he a police officer?

Tears brimmed her eyes. If he was, all she'd needed to do was stop and ask him for help, hide behind him, and he could've saved all of them. Giselle felt sick. Here she was, after all her efforts, after all her evasion and planning, back where she would've been if Serena had never warned her – in the hands of a child labor agent.

But Robert's free, she reminded herself and felt a flash of triumph. And the police officer might be stronger than Claude. There's still a chance! The guard was big and the officer had been tall and thin, but it wasn't always size that won battles. It was more the surprise she'd heard in the policeman's voice that made her wonder if he could subdue Claude. He'd been caught off guard.

An idea leapt into her mind. Maybe, just maybe, she could use the same tactic. A few moments ago, the shock of seeing a man on the road had kept her frozen long enough for him to grab her, so she knew first-hand how effective surprise could be. Maybe she too could use some swift and unexpected action to her advantage. If the agent would only relax his grip a bit or possibly become distracted by the fighting, it could be all she needed.

Domi. I am here. Oh no! He has her. We must help her!

I cannot hurt him in any way, but I can call for help. There are two men struggling in the forest. I hear them crashing in the undergrowth. Let us pray they will put aside their conflict to help your girl.

And if not? We will think of something, I promise. We will neither stand idly by nor give up. This evil man will not be allowed to steal her away. We will stop him, because we must – somehow.

Almost instantly, her chance came. His grip on her arm relaxed and Giselle kicked back as hard as she could. She felt momentarily pleased when her heel made contact with his shin, but her satisfaction was short-lived. The man swore and jerked upward on her arm as he tightened his grip over her mouth. But this time his hand covered her nose as well.

Giselle tried to inhale but she couldn't breathe. His hand was blocking all of her air passages. She closed her eyes and kicked back again, suddenly desperate. This time she missed.

He laughed softly but she hardly noticed. Her lungs were screaming for air! Stars exploded in front of her eyes and her efforts became more frantic – and less effective. A mist seemed to rise before her eyes and float in front of her. I'm going to die! The thought shrieked through her head. She kicked back again, but her attempt was feeble. She was losing strength fast.

"Help! Help!" The sharp sound ricocheted out of the night. Another girl was calling for help just a short distance away. The agent swung Giselle around to face the sound. Distracted, his grip on her mouth and nose loosened and Giselle sucked in the pure, sweet air. One deep breath. Two. Three. The fog lifted from her vision.

"Help! Please help!" the voice came again. Was this the girl who was supposed to take Robert to safety? But no, Giselle didn't think it was. This girl sounded different – older and not frightened.

The sound of struggle in the woods paused for a split second. Then another loud "oof" shot toward Giselle, followed by a groan, and the sound of someone treading through the underbrush toward them.

Giselle knew she had to do something – anything – and fast. There was a chance the man walking toward them was the policeman coming to help, but she didn't think so. She couldn't imagine him just walking

when someone was calling for help. And the agent's hand over her mouth had relaxed even more. He thought it was the guard too.

Sheer desperation lent Giselle strength as she bit down on the flesh of the agent's palm. At the same time, she drove her free elbow back into his stomach and then kicked back, a little higher this time, and made contact with his kneecap. Once! Twice!

The man cried out and jerked his hand from her face. His grip on her arm loosened for an instant and Giselle twisted away and kicked again. She was free!

Without wasting a millisecond, she rocketed into the darkness on the other side of the road, away from the approaching guard, away from the agent's grasping hands and the girl calling for help.

She sent a silent thank you back to the unknown girl who had distracted her captor, but didn't slow her headlong flight. She had Robert to think of now. And besides, there was nothing she could do. If she tried to help the girl, the men would just catch her again. And what help could she be then, for either the girl or for Robert? She could only hoped her savior had had enough time to escape as well.

As the pain subsided, the man strode to the edge of the road. He could hear the girl moving swiftly away from him – too swiftly. There was no way he'd catch her in the dark, not unless he was able to surprise her again.

Suddenly he remembered the plea for help and ran in the direction of the voice. The road was empty. He could hear his partner lumbering through the bush. "Claude! Hurry up!" the man yelled.

"Coming, Boss." Claude stepped onto the road.

"What happened?" the man asked in an angry voice. "Did you get him?"

Claude was breathing hard from exertion. "Yeah." He wiped sweat from his forehead. "He's tied up. I need to find some rope so I can get my belt back."

"Did he get a good look at you?"

Claude looked up at the moon. "Don't know," he said, his voice worried. "Maybe."

"We better get moving, then. We'll stop on the way out of town and get the money back I paid for the girl." He walked to where he'd left the machete and bent to pick it up. "We got to get them kids out of here before morning."

"Uh, Boss," said Claude, not moving.

The agent turned back to see Claude looking down at the ground and shuffling his feet in the dirt. "What?" His voice was hard.

"I think they might be gone," Claude said, looking up. "I heard them at the back of the shed."

"What do you mean?" the man barked. He tapped the machete against his leg and leaned toward the guard.

The guard flinched away. "They must've bent that rusty tin back, or something. I heard them, and then I saw some of them running. I chased them and that's when I ran into that cop."

54

"They couldn't get out. I checked that shed. It was strong. And the girl you were chasing was the runaway."

"Maybe it was a trick, then," the guard suggested with sudden hope. "The door was tied shut, but..."

The men didn't waste any time. They ran to the shed – to find the door wide open. The agent screamed in rage and kicked at the tin wall. The sound vibrated through the forest. He turned to the guard with a roar and waved the machete in his face. "You're such an idiot! She tricked you! That brat tricked you! They didn't escape out the back. She led you away and they cut the rope from inside!" The agent suddenly fell into a speechless rage and began to pace wildly back and forth, his movements frenzied.

"Uh, sorry, Boss." Claude stood with his head lowered and waited patiently. He'd seen the rages before and knew they passed quickly. And afterward, there would be lots of things to do, lots of orders to follow.

The agent stopped abruptly, and his voice was deadly calm as he spoke. "There were two of them on the road. We can bet more ran that way. We're going to catch them – all of them. You understand? No matter how long it takes, we're going to catch them."

The guard nodded meekly.

"But first we'll take care of that cop." The agent turned to look in the policeman's direction. "We can't have him complicating things. We've got to bribe him, pay him to not say anything. Hey, maybe he'll even help us catch them."

He smiled at the irony of the situation. They could use the cop to lure the kids in. They'd come running because they'd think they were being saved.

And if the cop refused to cooperate? Well, they'd make him. It might take a little time to convince him, but he had no choice – if he wanted to stay healthy.

But then, why waste the time? They could just take his uniform and pretend to be him. That would be even simpler.

The police officer is unconscious. Quickly, we must move him. We must hide him before they come back. Help me, Domi. Let me lay him across your back. He cannot be left here. He would be at their mercy. And I do not believe they have any mercy to give.

We will go to your girl soon, I promise. As soon as we can.

Giselle raced through the bushes. She had a good head start, but she knew it wouldn't take the men long to regroup. They'd soon be after her. And when she had her brother with her, safe and sound, they'd need as much of a head start as possible. Robert couldn't run very fast. Five-year-olds weren't known for their speed, especially compared to grown men.

After the longest time, the bridge took shape against the moonlit sky. Giselle came to a quick stop. What if the men were waiting for her beneath the gray stone arch? The thought was unreasonable – there was no way they could know the bridge was the prearranged meeting place – but her breath quickened as her eyes searched the shadows beneath.

If only I had a light, she thought. As if the night could read her thoughts and was conspiring against her, a passing cloud suddenly concealed the moon. Intense darkness swamped the terrain. Giselle could hardly see her hand in front of her face.

What do I do now? But she knew what she had to do. There was no point in even wasting time thinking about it. She had to go forward. She took a single step into the blackness. Nothing grabbed her. She took another step. And another. A twig snapped beneath her foot. She stopped, her heart in her throat.

She thought she was near enough to touch the bridge and reached out. The stone was cold beneath her fingers. "Robert?" It was the softest whisper. She stood silent for a long moment. "Robert? Are you there? It's Giselle."

There was a sudden explosion of movement and a small form launched from beneath the bridge. The creature hit her mid-thigh and wrapped thin arms around her legs. A sob burst around her.

Giselle choked back her cry of surprise. She recognized the sob and the strength in the skinny body. "Shhh," she murmured, and put her hand on Robert's back. "Hush now. It's okay. I'm here."

57

Another sob. Giselle's eyes shot up to the edge of the bridge. "You have to be quiet, Robert." She loosened her little brother's arms from around her legs, knelt before him, and lifted him up into her arms. "Are you okay? Did they hurt you?" she said in her softest voice.

"They scared me, Zellie."

"Where's the girl who brought you here?"

"She had to go with the others. She said you'd come get me."

The hoarseness in his voice told Giselle he'd been crying a long time. Instant fury flared up inside her. This was her aunt's fault. She'd done this horrible thing to them both.

"What're we going to do, Zellie?" whispered Robert. He sounded slightly calmer.

Giselle took a deep breath. Her presence was making him feel safe. He didn't need to see any expression of her anger. Robert needed one person in his life he could count on to be strong and dependable. She would be that person. "We're going to find a new home, Robert," she whispered. "Just you and me, where no one can hurt us again."

"Promise, Zellie?"

She paused for just a moment and put a gentle hand on his cheek. It was too dark to see his eyes, but she knew she'd be looking into their chocolate-colored depths if she could see him. "I promise," she said, fervently. And she'd never meant anything more in her life.

Rage encompassed the man once again when they discovered the policeman was gone. It was all he could do to not strike at Claude. His partner had lost the cop and let the children escape. He was worse than an idiot! Letting a little girl get the best of him!

With a supreme effort, the man controlled his fury. Claude was the only one who would help him. Now if he could find a way to make the man useful. He needed a new plan: first, a way to recapture the children, and then a way to pay Claude back for his incompetence.

But more than anything, he wanted to catch that cursed girl. She was the one who'd caused all this trouble. Everything, all that had happened, was her fault. And she would pay the most of all.

The policeman should be safe here, in this tranquil grove. The surrounding brush is thick. The trees are tall and sheltering. I do not think the wicked man will look for him in this thicket.

I will ask the wild ones to stay away from him as well, to let him rest peacefully. He is still unconscious, but I believe he will wake in a few hours. And when he does, I am sure he will have a terrible headache. Thankfully, it will be no worse than that.

Now Domi, let us go find your girl. We must hurry. I feel a terrible tension in my heart and I believe she is in grave danger — or will be soon — more danger than she has yet seen this night.

Come, we must hurry.

Giselle crawled under the stone arch. She knew they should move on, but she was so tired. Beneath the bridge seemed a safe place to hide, just for a minute or two. She leaned back against the cool stone and pulled Robert onto her lap. The little boy snuggled against her, and she wrapped her arms around his shivering body.

Now that she had her little brother with her, she needed to start on the next phase of her plan. They would go back for Domi – and then what? Telling Robert she would create a safe home for him was a lot different from actually doing it. Where could they go? What would they do?

We could go to the Mont des Enfants Perdus, she thought. She liked the name of that mountain. The Mountain of Lost Children. She laid her cheek against the top of Robert's head. If any children were lost, she and Robert were.

But it's different now than when I was thinking of going to the mountains alone, she realized. What if I can't find enough food for Robert in the wilderness? And can I find or build a home that'll keep us safe from humans and wild animals? She shuddered. Or from worse? There were recent rumors of zombies living on the Mont des Enfants Perdus. Could they be true?

Maybe we should go to the city instead, she considered. There, they could at least hide among all the other homeless people, all the other orphans. But finding enough food for Robert in a place where she would have to compete for every scrap would be almost impossible. She'd heard that destitute children were forced to steal there, just to eat. What if Robert grew up to be a thief?

If only she had another option – almost any option would do. Her mind turned reluctantly back to the whistling man. What if they went back and begged him and his wife to take them in?

Stop it! she commanded herself. That won't work. Aunty will just come to get us, or the child labor agent will come. If the man even says yes, which he won't! Tears brimmed in her eyes. There was no use thinking of ever having a happy, normal family again. It would never happen.

Robert's breath had become slow and deep. Giselle shifted him a little on her lap, relieved he was able to sleep. She would have no such luxury this night. Long before dawn touched the sky, she would have to make her decision. But how could she? How could she choose when the results of her decision would alter their lives forever? Her choice would actually dictate the kind of man Robert would grow to be.

Giselle stared into the darkness, her eyes haunted. In her mind, the future spread before her like a blank canvas, and the only things she could think to paint on it were horrifying.

The men are right behind us, following her trail as well. The lead man is a very good tracker, even though the batteries in his flashlight are low. We are fortunate, Domi. If the beam were brighter, he might see us. We must go faster, and do it soundlessly, without leaving sign of our passing.

You say she is there, beneath the bridge? You can smell her scent. And someone is with her, someone you do not know.

We must get her away from this trap, as quickly as we can. We have no time to lose. They are almost upon us.

Giselle leaned her head back against the cold stone. Maybe if she rested a little longer, the decision would become clear. She could spare a few more minutes. The men didn't know she was there – if they were looking for her at all. She shut her eyes.

"Hello? Domi's girl?"

The voice was gentle but Giselle almost leapt out of her skin. Robert woke with a start. "Zellie?" he murmured, his mind still clouded with sleep.

"Who's there?" Giselle's voice trembled. Robert whimpered on her lap.

"Come with me. Hurry. There is no time to explain."

"Who are…?"

A soft nicker interrupted her.

"Domi?" Giselle's mouth dropped open. "Madame Celeste? But how…"

"Hurry," the voice said again, more insistently. "They are coming."

Giselle needed no more encouragement. She crawled from under the bridge with Robert right behind her. When she straightened, her eyes fastened on the pony's pale silhouette. It was Domi! But the form standing at his side was much smaller than Madame Celeste. "Come," the girl whispered. "Climb onto his back."

She's the girl on the road, Giselle realized, suddenly recognizing the voice. The one who called for help! She lifted Robert onto the pony's thin back and sprang up behind him. The girl melted into the night before them, and the pony stepped eagerly after her. Swiftly, they moved away from the bridge.

Suddenly, the night seemed unnaturally quiet. Giselle could hear the soft sound Domi made moving through the undergrowth, and the crackling of something heavy stumbling through the bushes behind them. It took her a moment to realize that the drums had finally ceased.

Abruptly the noises behind them stopped as well, and men's voices took their place. Were they at the bridge? Fear constricted Giselle's chest, and she tightened her arms around her brother. They'd almost been caught! She bent to whisper in the little boy's ear, "Don't say anything, Robert. Nothing at all." His body moved in her arms as he nodded his head.

The voices faded quickly in the distance. They were leaving the men behind. Soon Giselle could hear nothing but Domi walking through the bushes. Even the girl in front was as silent as a shadow. Giselle drew a deep, relaxing breath. Once again, the mysterious girl had saved her, and this time Robert too. She owed her everything – her and Robert's lives, even.

"Try to sleep," she whispered to her little brother. "I'll hold you onto Domi's back."

The little boy laid his head against her arm. "Night, Zellie," he murmured.

Giselle felt his body relax against hers, and within minutes, his soft rhythmic breath eased around her. With her brother safe in her arms, Giselle's thoughts turned back to the shadowy person who walked in front of them. Who was she? Where did she come from? How did she know Domi? And how did she know they needed help?

There were no answers, yet a warm feeling spread through Giselle's body. Someone had cared enough to help her and Robert. They were not alone after all.

✛ ✛ ✛ ✛ ✛ ✛

The night had long been silent and Robert long asleep when Giselle heard movement coming from behind them. She held her breath and listened. A twig snapped. Something brushed against some leaves.

"Someone's following us," she whispered to the girl. It was the darkest time of night now, just before dawn, and Giselle wasn't even sure the girl was still there. She couldn't hear her, and all she could see was the faint glimmer of Domi's light gray withers, neck, and ears as he walked steadily onward.

"Yes, I know." The girl's voice floated back to her. "There is no need to worry."

Giselle tried to relax but it was impossible. Trying not to disturb Robert, she craned her neck around. Everything behind Domi was

66

saturated by night. She couldn't see a thing. But she could hear, and the sounds were becoming more definite. Some thing – no – some things were following them.

She swallowed nervously and looked up at the star-studded sky. If only the moon hadn't set. Or dawn would hurry and come. Despite her best efforts, a vision of the restavec agent and the guard, reaching to grab her, leapt into her mind. But that's stupid, she chided herself. These sounds are different. Maybe its wild animals! Or zombies! This thought sent a jolt of terror down Giselle's spine, and her arms tightened around Robert.

"Mama," he muttered in his sleep.

Giselle forced herself to loosen her hold and take a deep, calming breath. If whatever's following us wanted to attack, it would've done it by now, she rationalized. There's no reason to panic. I hope.

She'd foiled them at the bridge, having taken off just moments before they got there. He knew they'd almost caught her because the ground was still slightly warm where she'd been resting.

Then, after the bridge, she'd become more difficult to track – at least until he saw the pony's hoof prints and realized she was riding. This girl was clever. Somehow finding a pony to ride. Could it be the one from the canvas shack? But when he'd seen her in town, she didn't have a pony with her. It didn't make sense.

The irritation of failing flashlight batteries interrupted his thoughts. Finally, when the light became too weak to see by, they were forced to stop and wait for daylight. The agent ripped some branches from the nearby bushes, shook them to rid them of any unwanted creatures, and made himself a bed. He lay down and wrapped his arms around himself for warmth, thankful the guard was still too ashamed to say much.

The agent listened as Claude tossed and turned, then he rolled over and tried to shut out the noise. He was tired, more so than he'd been for a long while, and he needed the rest. Tomorrow was going to be a long day.

But even after Claude started snoring, he couldn't sleep. It was the girl's fault. He had too many questions about her, questions with no answers.

When he finally drifted off it was to dream of the girl – running, looking back, and beckoning him on. When he finally caught her, she was whispering to the black dog. He went up to grab her, but she slipped out of his grasp. The dog started barking.

And suddenly the man realized it wasn't barking, it was laughing at him. And then the girl was laughing too. And the pony stood behind them, laughing as well. Even Claude was there, pointing at him and calling him a coward. Mocking him. It was not a restful sleep.

The night was quickly fading away. When Giselle could make out the shadowy form of the girl walking in front of Domi, she turned to look behind again.

They were being followed – but not by men, wild animals, or zombies. The shadowy forms behind them were small and thin. A whisper reached her ear. A child's voice. They were being followed by children. It took only moments for Giselle to realize who the children were – the escaped restavecs. Somehow, though it seemed impossible, they'd found her, Domi, Robert, and the strange girl in the dark of night and followed them to safety.

When the new sun peeked over the horizon, the fiery light caught their leader and her hair lit up like a flare in the sudden brightness. Giselle's eyes opened wide in surprise. She'd never seen hair so beautiful! And she could tell she wasn't alone in her amazement. From behind her came soft exclamations of awe.

"Hey, who are you?" she called out. "What's your name?"

The girl glanced back – and Giselle's arms tightened around Robert again. The strange girl's eyes were the color of molten gold, a vibrant rich color that glowed from deep within. "My name is Angelica," she said and turned again to stride through the brush. Domi stepped after her without hesitation.

Giselle didn't know what to say. This girl was the one who'd saved her last night, twice, and she couldn't help but trust her – but she looked so incredibly different from anyone Giselle had seen before, all gold and ivory, like a creature from another world.

A sudden thought made her gasp and she looked back. The children were now clearly visible in the morning light. And thankfully, they looked like almost every other child Giselle had ever seen. She smiled at the boy closest to her and he smiled back. The girl behind him raised her hand in a small wave.

"Zellie? Where are we?"

"I don't know, Robert," she answered. And she didn't. Everything around them was completely unfamiliar. She'd never been here before. There weren't any houses or roads or any other signs of civilization. Bushes and trees, hills and canyons, stretched away in every direction. Mountains reached to the sky to either side of them.

Angelica must have heard Robert's question as well, for she walked back to Domi with a graceful step. Her fingers lingered across the pony's forehead as she spoke. "We are going someplace to rest," she said to Robert. Then she directed her gaze to the children standing behind. "We will be safe there, for a few hours at least," she added.

Giselle looked back. The children were staring, shocked, into Angelica's golden eyes. They weren't frightened that her hair was so bright – after all, they'd seen blonde people before – but they couldn't justify the girl's strange amber eyes. One of the youngest children, a scrawny girl that looked barely older than Robert, stumbled backward to slip her hand into that of a slightly taller girl. Giselle noticed that both girls were painfully thin. In fact, all the children were.

The poor things, thought Giselle. They need someone to take care of them – and Angelica's probably the only one who's ever tried. "Don't worry," she said, making her voice as reassuring as possible. "There's nothing to be afraid of. We're here to help you. Both of us."

"Yes," Angelica added, glancing at Giselle gratefully. "We are here to help. There is a building ahead, a deserted shack. We can rest there for a few hours, and then we must decide what we will do."

Giselle's lips tightened. The same question kept coming back. What were they going to do? And now the answer would be even more elusive. There were eight children to worry about, not just one. But at least she and Angelica had overcome their first hurdle – the children were relaxing. They seemed to accept the strange girl, at least for now.

And maybe after we get to the building, after I get some sleep, I'll be able to think of something, Giselle reasoned with renewed hope. Or Angelica will have some ideas.

The golden girl moved away and Domi started after her. "Just a minute," said Giselle, stopping them. She slipped from the pony's back and held her hand out to the smallest girl of all, walking at the end of the line. The child looked exhausted. "If you want, you can ride the pony," Giselle offered. She waited for the girl to come forward, then knelt in front of her. "What's your name?"

70

The girl kept her eyes on the ground and her voice was almost inaudible. "Amelie."

"I'm Giselle, and this is Domi. Would you like to ride him, Amelie?"

The little girl nodded, then looked up with hopeful eyes. A tentative smile touched her lips. Giselle lifted her behind her brother. "Hold on to Robert," she instructed. "And Robert, you grab Domi's mane. It's your job to keep as still as you can, so Amelie doesn't slip." The little boy nodded firmly and clutched a handful of mane. He was taking his new job seriously. "Thanks, buddy," Giselle whispered to the pony.

As they set out, she walked beside Angelica, leaving Domi and the children to follow. She hoped her actions would show there was nothing to fear from Angelica's strangeness – and it wasn't long before she felt a small hand in hers. She looked down to see a girl with scarred legs smiling up at her. She seemed to be around eight years old. "I'm Kristine," she said as she squeezed Giselle's hand. "I'm the one you talked to in the shed."

"I'm Giselle. Thanks for taking such good care of Robert," Giselle said and smiled back.

"I'm Mark," said a ten-year-old boy on Kristine's other side.

"The boy with the knife," said Giselle, and Mark nodded.

"I'm Paul," came a voice from behind Giselle.

She turned around to see a boy with a bruised face. He seemed to be only a year or so younger than she was. "Nice to meet you," she said.

"I'm Paris, and this is my little sister, Tyla." The two skinny girls looked almost identical, with one being only slighter taller than the other. "You said your names are Giselle and Angelica?"

"Yes," answered Angelica.

Giselle nodded as she cast her gaze around. Hadn't there been another child? Yes, there he was: a boy around seven years old, standing behind Domi. "What's your name?" she asked the boy.

"He never talks," volunteered Mark. "We don't know his name."

Angelica knelt and held her hand out to the child. "You're safe now, little one. You may tell us your name if you wish. Come forward."

Domi turned and gently pushed the boy toward Angelica with his muzzle. The boy went obediently, his eyes cast down. He stood and stared at the ground for a full minute, then uncertainly brushed his fingertips against her hand. Angelica didn't move and, a moment later, he placed his hand in hers.

71

Bird noises woke him suddenly, and moments later he was on his feet. The sun was already well above the horizon. They'd overslept!

The man kicked Claude's leg. "Get up!" he commanded.

Claude groaned, rolled onto his back and blinked a few times, and then sat up. Slowly, he climbed to his feet.

The man stalked off, his eyes roaming the ground. The trail would be much easier to follow in the daylight. They'd make good time, as long as the guard kept up.

Claude didn't follow him immediately. First he stretched and then he inhaled deeply, his head tipped back and eyes closed. Then he yawned and rubbed his eyes, stretched again, and finally followed his boss into the undergrowth.

They arrived at their destination, a tiny mud hut, an hour later. Giselle had never been so happy to stop. She'd had no sleep the night before, and that, combined with tremendous stress and exertion, made her absolutely exhausted.

She could hardly imagine how the smaller children felt. Even though some had probably slept a bit before she'd arrived to help them escape, they weren't as tough as she was. They would be close to collapse by now.

While Angelica made sure the mud hut was still safe, Giselle lifted Robert and Amelie from Domi's back. Then she led them inside the shelter. They let go of her hand to collapse onto a pile of straw next to the wall and cuddle up beside Kristine. Instantly their eyes shut. Giselle was about to lie down beside them when she heard her name. Paul was standing in the doorway, motioning to her to come. With a sigh, Giselle left the younger children to sleep.

Outside the shelter, Angelica looked up from massaging Domi's back as he grazed. "You both should rest," she said to Giselle and Paul. "We will have to move on in a couple hours."

"I'd rather know what we're going to do first," said Paul.

Though all she wanted to do was sleep, Giselle nodded in agreement.

The three sat in a circle on the dry ground. "What are the choices before us?" asked Angelica.

"We could go to the city," suggested Paul.

"Or stay here in the mountains," added Giselle. "But really neither are good choices. I've gone over it and over it."

Paul shook his head. "I don't want to stay here. There's no food, except what we can scrounge from the land."

"But the city isn't good for the little ones," Giselle said. "And it'll be hard for us to support them there too."

Paul didn't argue.

"Are there no other possibilities?" asked Angelica, her voice filled with concern.

"None I can think of," said Giselle.

"Me either," said Paul. He looked down at his hands and despair slumped his shoulders.

There was a rustling noise behind them and Giselle tensed. She twisted around to see the little boy who was too shy to tell his name standing in the doorway of the hut.

"Come join us," invited Angelica and held a pale hand toward the child. He came timidly forward, stopping between Angelica and Paul, his eyes locked on the golden girl in awe. "Do you have something you wish to say?" Angelica prompted.

The little boy nodded his head, but didn't open his mouth.

"We will not hurt you," added Angelica. "I promise. You may speak freely here."

The boy's voice was so quiet when he spoke that Giselle had to strain to hear him. "Children's Village," he said. "On the other side of the Mont des Enfants Perdus."

"But isn't that just a story?" asked Giselle. "It's not real, is it?"

"What's the Children's Village?" Paul asked Giselle.

"It's supposed to be a village where orphans live, near Port-au-Prince, I think. But I always assumed it was only a rumor." Bitterness saturated her voice. "No one wants to help orphans."

The little boy shook his head. "Maybe it is more than a rumor," Angelica suggested.

"Even if it's true, how could we get there?" asked Paul. "The only way is along the main road. The restavec agents would catch us, easy."

"We could keep traveling through the mountains," suggested Giselle, and then quickly amended, "If the village even exists, that is."

"But…" Paul stopped. He looked sheepishly at Giselle.

"What?" she asked.

"You know. The zombies. They live on the Mont des Enfants Perdus. Everyone says…" He stopped again, obviously afraid of looking like a coward to the others.

"Zombies aren't real. They don't exist," insisted Giselle, hoping the scorn in her voice would mask her own fear. "I mean, how can they? There's no such thing as dead people who can walk around. That's ridiculous."

"So we are decided," Angelica said suddenly. "We will go over the

74

Mont des Enfants Perdus to the Village of the Children. If the village does not exist, we can then re-evaluate our choices."

There was a long silence. Giselle fought to keep her eyes open. She had to think. How had they come to such a hasty, unclear decision? Trekking all the way across a wild mountain to find a village they didn't know existed? It sounded crazy – but she had nothing better to suggest. "Okay," she finally agreed.

"Okay," Paul said beside her. He sounded as doubtful as she did.

The little boy lowered himself to Angelica's lap and rested his head against her shoulder. He twisted a strand of golden hair around a finger and sighed deeply.

"Jon," he whispered. "My name is Jon."

After an hour of tedious tracking, the trail suddenly became easier to follow. Many small footprints marked the earth, and the agent's foul mood improved immensely. In fact, he felt positively jubilant. Somehow the brats had found each other in the dark and were now running in a group. There was no need to go searching all over creation to round them up. He laughed silently. Even stupid Claude could track them now, though not as expertly, to be sure.

His face became hard again. When he had them, the first thing he'd do would be make an example of the girl in front of the others. He'd show them what would happen if they ever ran away again.

After all, they needed to learn submission if they were to make good restavecs, and it was part of his job to deliver them to his patrons already trained.

Giselle fell into a dark, dreamless sleep the second her head touched the straw. It seemed only moments later when she felt something gently touch her shoulder. She was awake instantly and leapt to her feet, her heart pounding like crazy. She relaxed when she saw Angelica standing before her, holding out a half coconut shell.

"I am sorry to wake you so abruptly," the older girl said. "We must go soon. But first, here is some water."

Giselle rubbed her eyes and sat up. The water felt wonderful in her parched throat, cold and clear. When she'd drained every drop, she handed the half shell back to Angelica. " Thanks," she said. "How long have I been asleep?"

"For less than two hours, I am afraid," said Angelica.

"It didn't seem nearly that long."

"We must wake the others. Our pursuers are only two miles away. I doubled back on our trail and saw them in the distance. They are quickly advancing."

Giselle and Angelica didn't waste any time. Within a couple minutes, the children were awake and drinking their fill of the water Angelica had found while they were sleeping.

Giselle lifted Robert and Amelie onto Domi's back. Angelica whispered to the pony, and then turned to Tyla. "Would you like to ride with the others?" she asked gently.

"It's too much for him to carry," Tyla said, although she looked longingly at the pony.

"He wishes to carry you as well."

The little girl hesitated for a moment, and then nodded her head. "Just for a little way, then," she consented, and Giselle lifted her onto Domi's back to ride behind Amelie.

Angelica turned to Giselle when the troop was ready. "You go ahead," she said. "I will clear away the signs of our presence here."

Worry flashed in Giselle's eyes. She pulled Angelica a short distance away, and then glanced back at the children. They were talking among themselves. "But Angelica, I don't know which way to go," she whispered.

"I do not know the path either, but surely there is a way over the mountain. I can help you find it when I am done here."

Giselle nodded. "Okay, but hurry," she said. "And be careful. You can't let them catch you."

"I will be careful," Angelica nodded. "I promise."

Giselle led the children away from the hut. There was no need to remind them to be quiet. They knew what was at stake. The only sound was the rustle of leaves as they passed, the patter of Domi's hooves, and the whisper of callused soles over the earth. At the top of the first small rise, Giselle turned back for a quick look. Angelica was sweeping the ground in front of the hut with a leafy branch, erasing their tracks. When they reached the top of the second incline, Giselle could see only forest behind.

The irregular terrain and unchecked undergrowth were difficult to walk through, and Giselle was impressed with how well the children were doing. She knew how tired they were – she was too – yet they were making good time. But when she saw the next brushy, rock-strewn slope, she almost groaned aloud. It was so steep!

Paul can lead the way up, and I'll help the stragglers, she decided. That's probably the fastest way over.

The ascent was going well until Paul almost reached the top. Only halfway up herself, Giselle saw him breathing heavily as he paused to look down at them. Then, one by one, Mark, Kristine, and Jon reached him and stopped as well. Even Domi stopped beside the exhausted group.

"Come on, guys. We have to keep going," gasped Giselle when she'd finally pulled Paris up the slope to stand beside them.

"Look, Giselle," said Paul. He pointed down the hillside. "What do we do?"

Giselle turned. From their vantage point, they could see the hut again. Angelica's hair gleamed like a golden mane as she continued to sweep away the tracks the children had left. And on the other side of the shack, two dark figures moved quickly toward the unwary girl.

If we can see the men, they can see us, Giselle realized with a start. All they have to do is look up!

"Into the trees. Quick!" she said, her voice hushed and insistent. The children and Domi scrambled the rest of the way up the incline and dashed into the shadowy forest. Giselle was the last to reach the safety of the trees. She sent Paris on with the others and looked back.

Should she roll a rock down the hill? Angelica might realize the sound was meant as a warning – or it might distract her and allow the men to sneak up on her.

What else can I do? I can't yell, because then they'll know where we are. But I can't just let them sneak up on her either!

The men were almost to the hut now. Giselle's breath quickened as she watched Angelica lay her sweeping branch on the ground and walk away from the shack in the opposite direction. The girl glanced back at the hut just before disappearing into the heavy undergrowth. Moments later, the men walked around the shack and bent over the girl's footprints.

She knew they were there all along, Giselle suddenly realized. And she purposefully laid a false trail for them! She smiled. Angelica was smart. She'd not only erased the children's tracks, but had made some new, fresh ones – tracks that would lead their pursuers in the wrong direction.

Giselle faded back into the forest. "She's safe," she said to the children gathered round. "And she's leaving them an obvious trail to follow – away from us." There was murmur of relief and admiration. "We'll go faster if you keep in front, Paul," added Giselle, looking at the young boy.

Paul stood a little taller and nodded. "Let's go," he said and led off. The others quickly fell in behind. Giselle came last in line, but this time not only to help the slower children. If the restavec agents did find their trail again, she wanted to be the first to know.

I hope they will follow my tracks away from the children. And there is something else I'd like to try. If they think I am trying to keep them from following my trail, they may be convinced it is the right one.

Someone had been inside the hut. He could see fresh indentations in the straw where they'd rested. It could only have been the kids. If only he hadn't slept in, they might have caught them.

The man gritted his teeth as Claude lowered his large body to the ground and leaned against the mud wall. The guard pulled a cigarette pack from his pocket and put one of the white sticks in his mouth.

"There's no time for that," the man spat at him.

Claude appraised him with cold eyes, then took the cigarette from his mouth and slid it back in the pack with the others.

The agent snorted and turned away to follow the single set of footprints going off into the bush. He'd noticed right away that the tracks were from feet too big for the younger children. There are some scuffs, though. Maybe the kids went this way and then that girl had wiped out their tracks. And then didn't erase her own? Would she be that sloppy? She knew what was at stake and, so far, she'd been quite clever.

She's tired, he reasoned. And it was possible she hadn't known her pursuers were so close. Maybe they'd caught her by surprise and she didn't have time to wipe out her own footprints. Or she was leading them astray while the brats escaped in another direction.

He followed the tracks into the bush. The trail was unchanged, except for – he stopped abruptly. What was that, glittering in the morning light? A filament of spun gold? A glistening spider web? It was strung chest-high, from one bush to another, right across the girl's tracks.

"It's a hair," said Claude, looking over his shoulder.

"It can't be. Who would it come from?

"The pony? Maybe it's a palomino or something."

The agent leaned close to the strand. Was it the pony's hair? It seemed too fine, like a strand of flaxen silk. And he'd never seen a horse with a mane or tail that color. Palomino manes and tails were white, not gold.

With a puzzled expression, he poked at the filament with the machete. A warm tingle buzzed against his hand. He jerked away with a gasp and glanced back, embarrassed that Claude had heard his surprise. The shame didn't last. When he saw Claude's face twist in held-back laughter, his own face hardened. He turned to grab the golden thread between his thumb and forefinger.

But it was gone! He stared at the branches it had been caught on, at first thinking he must not be seeing it because it was so fine. There was no sign of the filament on the ground either.

So it was magic! Another trick played on them by that girl. But the magic wasn't strong, and as the girl got farther from them, she was less able to maintain her illusions. That had to be why the strand disappeared.

"Uh, Boss," Claude spoke hesitantly behind him. "There's another one."

A jolt of fear invaded him when he noticed the glimmering thread, just a few yards ahead.

Slowly, he backed away. He didn't know what the girl was trying to do, but there was one way to find out. They would go back to the hut and look for more tracks. If they found them, and if there were more than one set of footprints, they would follow them. If there weren't any other tracks, they would come back and follow these, despite the magical threads.

He spun around, almost driving the machete blade into Claude's leg. "We'll separate and go in widening circles around the hut," he instructed the guard as they walked. "See if there's another set of tracks. If she's trying to lure us in the wrong direction, we'll find out when we do the circles."

As soon as they reached the hut, Claude pulled his cigarette pack out again.

"Not now!" barked the agent. He snatched the guard's matches and flung them into the bushes.

Claude glared at him for a moment, then stalked to the left without a word, his massive shoulders stiff with resentment.

My plan did not work, but the fear I saw in the man's eyes has given me another idea. I will leave the magical hairs across the children's real trail. If the restavec agent truly is afraid, he will turn back again.

They do not know I exist yet, and that gives me an advantage as well. In fact, I believe they think Giselle is doing this — and we may be able to use that against them too, later on, if I cannot turn them back now.

"Over here, Boss!" Claude's yell burst through the quiet like a bull's bellow.

The man made his way to the guard's side in seconds. When he saw the trail, he was impressed that Claude had even noticed it. He wouldn't have expected the big man to know that the subtle scuffs in the dirt were the children's trail. Claude wasn't known for his brains.

The head agent examined the tracks. Five or six children had passed this way. And there were hoof prints. The rest of the children must be riding the pony. "Let's go," he muttered and strode along the trail.

Claude waited a few moments before following.

Giselle's legs burned as she climbed up, up, up, pulling Jon and Paris along with her. They'd been climbing one slope after another as they walked alongside the mountain, and she was almost ready to drop. Every movement needed energy she didn't have. But still, she somehow took another step. And another. And then another.

It didn't help that they weren't following a trail either. It took far more energy to walk through the bush – but it would also make them harder to track if the men turned around. At the top of the incline, Paris collapsed on the ground. Then Jon was down beside her, breathing heavily.

"We have to keep going," Giselle said, though she was glad to stop as well, if only for a moment. "I know you're tired, but we can't give up. If they've found our trail, they'll be gaining on us." If only she had some water to give them. A cool drink would make them all feel better. But she had nothing left to give, not even enough energy to pull them to their feet. Paris tipped onto her side in the dirt, curled into a ball, and closed her almond shaped eyes.

"We can take turns riding and walking," Giselle suggested, and then added in the firmest voice she could muster, "We can't stop. Come on, Paris. Get up."

With the promise of a ride on the pony's back, both Paris and Jon staggered to their feet. Paul and Giselle lifted Amelie, Robert, and Tyla from Domi's back and put Paris and Jon in their place, and the group trudged onward once more.

The agent came to a quick halt. "Look. On that branch." He pointed.

Claude moved closer and squinted. "It's another hair." He reached past the man to take it in his fingers. "Hey! It's gone! What the…" He blinked a couple of times. "It was there, wasn't it? It weren't my imagination?"

The agent shook his head. Claude was so thick-headed. Hadn't he noticed the other filaments had disappeared too? But maybe the guard's intelligence, or rather lack of intelligence, was an opportunity. The agent didn't want to go blundering through the golden filaments himself, just in case they were enchanted. But if Claude went first, he could clear the cursed fibers out of their way and collect the bad magic onto himself.

"I think they're spider webs that the sunlight makes look gold," he said. "And that they break easy, that's all."

"Sure. That's it," said Claude, but he didn't sound very convinced.

The agent stepped back. "I've been tracking them this whole time while you've just been lazing along behind. The trail's easy to follow now, so I'm taking a break. You go first." He pushed the guard forward. "Hurry up. I'll be right behind you."

This new ploy helped the children gain only a short distance. I must think of another plan. There must be something I can use.

I know. The large man is leading them now, and maybe he is not as good a tracker. Maybe he can be misled from the children's true path.

A few minutes later, Paul found a faint animal trail and started to follow it. At first, Giselle wondered if she should question his decision – she wasn't sure that following a trail, no matter how unused it might appear, was a good idea. If they were being followed, they'd now be far easier to track. But on the other hand, the children were hardly moving any-more. Maybe anything that helped them walk faster would be good.

I'll keep a better lookout. As long as we have enough warning, we'll be okay, she decided. She gazed back when they reached the top of yet another small rise. As far as she could see, the mountainside was deserted. There was no movement anywhere. Did that mean Angelica had succeeded? Had she led the men astray?

Or had she been caught?

The man cringed inwardly as Claude approached each golden strand. He made sure to keep well back, just in case something happened. There was no doubt in the agent's mind that the filaments were enchanted, and he almost pitied the big oaf of a guard. The bad magic Claude was collecting could be huge. But better the guard than himself.

Claude bent down to inspect the earth, and then straightened. "They went this way for sure," he grunted and strode ahead. The agent hunkered down to look at the ground. Yes, there were tracks, but they were hard to read. He could see one larger footprint, but the rest were unrecognizable after being stepped on by the guard's big, bumbling feet.

Soon he would take the lead again – but not until he was sure no more strange golden threads blocked their path. Others might laugh at how superstitious he was, but he knew both bizarre and evil omens existed in the world. Sometimes it was hard to tell which phenomenon could hurt you and which was merely strange, and he preferred not to take chances.

He smirked. Apparently Claude, in his simple innocence, was not as suspicious. Or more likely, he was just plain stupid. Either way, at least Claude was finally being useful.

My new plan is working! By jumping back and forth, leaving additional scuffmarks and tracks, I am leading them away from the children!

As long as I go swiftly enough that they do not see me, I should be able to lead them far, far away, and the children will continue on in safety.

At first Giselle felt only a strange, undefined niggling in her mind. Then, despite being exhausted, she jumped when a bird's high call rang around her. Yet it still wasn't until she saw a flicker of movement from behind a cluster of bushes that she realized something was watching them.

She froze, and her eyes raked the leafy branches. She couldn't see anything now. Should she approach? What if something jumped out at her? It couldn't possibly be the men, but what if it was another predator – or a zombie? Giselle was helpless to stop the idea from leaping into her mind again. Zombies had always been her greatest fear. The thought of them just seemed so horrible: ordinary people who'd died and been buried, then raised in the dead of night to walk again. The image of them, staggering jerkily and untiringly on and on, and doing whatever hideous things crossed their lifeless minds, sent revulsion and fear spinning through her body.

But what if there was someone who needed her behind the bushes, like a frightened, injured animal? Or another child? She picked up a stone and lobbed it into the undergrowth, and heard only the rock hitting the ground.

Slowly Giselle crept forward a few yards. She stopped when she could see inside the thicket. Thank goodness, there was nothing there. She moved her gaze over the mountainside. Heat shimmered below, and she could hear the bird again, but there was no other sign of life. And the feeling of being watched was gone.

It was probably a wild burro or a goat, Giselle concluded.

"Zellie?" The voice was quietly desperate.

Giselle spun around to see her brother slump to the ground. "Paul, stop," Giselle yelled and rushed to Robert's side.

Her brother looked up at her with dark, forlorn eyes. "I'm sorry, Zellie," he said. "I can't walk no more."

92

"Sure you can," said Giselle gently, and she lifted him to his feet. He fell against her, his small body quaking with exhaustion. She looked up to see three more of the children on the ground.

"Okay, you can sit for a minute, Robert," she relented and helped him down, then walked toward the head of the line. She patted Domi on the way. The pony's drooping head and splayed ears showed how worn-out he was as well. He needed a break as much as the children did.

"Maybe we should rest for a while," she said to Paul. She cast her gaze about, and then pointed up the hillside to a narrow, dark opening. "In that cave." She was surprised at how confident she sounded. "You take the children up there and I'll erase your tracks, leave a false trail, and double back. I'll look for water too. We're going to need some more soon."

Paul nodded, too tired to speak, and climbed through the bushes toward the cave opening. Giselle lifted Jon and Paris from Domi's back, and then hurried back to Robert. "Just follow Paul," she said. "He'll take you someplace you can rest for a while. Domi and I will be back soon."

"Okay, Zellie," Robert said and struggled to his feet. He was the last in line, and Giselle almost cried as she watched him labor up the short slope. The poor little guy! Why did life have to be so hard for him – for all of them? Paul stopped just short of the cave mouth and helped the smaller children the last few steps. By the time Giselle had found a good sweeping frond, they had all disappeared inside the shady alcove.

Within minutes, the children's tracks to the cave were obliterated and Giselle and Domi were hurrying along the faint trail. She felt more energetic than she had all morning, walking alone with the pony. "How are you doing, Domi?" she said to the little gray. He nickered in response. He seemed to have revived a bit as well, now free of his load of children.

They traversed the trail for some time before Giselle saw the perfect place to mislead their pursuers – a rockslide stretching from the bluff above, over the trail, and down the mountainside. It was the ideal place to double back. The men would know the children hadn't gone past the slide, but they wouldn't be able to track them on the rocks, and it would take them time to check both up and down the mountain. It was even possible they might never find where Giselle and Domi left the slide, as she planned to sweep their tracks away. Carefully, she led the way up into the jumbled rocks.

Sweat poured down her face as she climbed. Domi found the footing difficult, and they had to go slowly. The sun beat down mercilessly, unobstructed by branches or bushes, and soaked into the stones around them, making heat rise from beneath them as well. Now, even more than a rest, Giselle longed for a drink of water. She was getting so thirsty!

Halfway up the slide, Giselle led Domi off the rocks. She left him in the shade, grazing, and went back to sweep away their tracks. It took longer than she thought. Hoof prints were harder to sweep away than children's footprints. However, by the time she got back to the grove of trees, she was confident no one could tell where they'd left the slide.

"It's done, buddy," she said to the pony when she reached his side. Domi whinnied softly as Giselle laid her head on his bony withers. She felt like she could almost fall asleep right there, leaning on her friend. Except – she tensed. Something, or someone, was watching them again.

Still leaning on Domi, Giselle narrowed her eyes to a sliver. Everything became instantly blurry. It was a trick she'd learned in watching for her aunt's approach. She would appear unaware, as if she was resting or sleeping, and yet would easily see movement. Her eyes ranged slowly back and forth along the slit between her eyelids. And something moved! Her eyes popped open.

A face stared back at her from between two branches! A woman! Before Giselle could gasp in astonishment, the woman had disappeared.

For a moment, Giselle was frozen in shock, but then their need un-loosed her tongue. "Help us," she called out. "Don't go. We need help!" There was no response. "Please, don't go!" She caught a sob before it escaped from her throat. "Please," she said, and then her voice dropped to a whisper. "Don't go."

It was no use. The woman was gone. She and Domi were alone once again.

The agent could barely endure the pace. Claude was so slow, lumbering along like an ox. And the golden filaments didn't seem to be bothering him. Maybe it was safe to take the lead again. If he were in front again, they'd go much faster.

Claude stopped abruptly and bent over the tracks.

The man looked ahead. He couldn't see any magical threads. "Get out of my way," he commanded, unable to wait any longer. The guard let him by, and the agent strode along the obvious trail.

He'd only gone a few yards when something began to bother him. He bent to examine the footprints more closely. There were plenty of them, both full and partial footprints. So what was wrong? The answer came quickly. They were too uniform in size, as if the same two feet had made them all. And there was no sign of the pony's tracks.

Another wave of rage flowed over him. The girl had tricked them again! No, not him. Claude!

He spun around, shoved the surprised guard out of the way, and stalked back the way they'd come. They walked in stony silence until the agent couldn't hold in his anger any longer. He let loose a string of curses. Claude was an idiot! A stupid oaf! Allowing himself to be misled by a girl! How could he be so dense? So dimwitted?

At first, Claude followed meekly, looking sheepishly at the ground. The man didn't notice. Nor did he notice when the guard's face became thoughtful. Or when Claude's hands clenched into fists. Completely unaware, he strode back the way they'd come, abusive words falling behind him like leaves in autumn.

They lost much time following me. I hope Giselle and the children were able to travel far.

I must go to them, hone in on Domi's presence to find them, and see what more I can do to help.

Giselle led Domi back toward the cave along a natural ledge that ran along the base of the cliff. She listened for water falling, hoping to hear some tumbling over rocks or gurgling down below, but there was nothing.

When she reached the cave, she paused. It looked different than she remembered. Hadn't the entrance been narrower? She walked inside to find an empty chamber.

It's a different cave, Giselle realized. She inhaled deeply. She should continue on – but the coolness in the cave felt so refreshing. She relaxed against the rock wall, reveling in the chill air.

A soft whinny came from outside, and then the sound of a hoof striking stone. Giselle rallied herself. "I'm coming, Domi," she said. "You're right. We need to get going." Reluctantly, she stepped back into the hot afternoon and kissed the pony on his forehead.

"Giselle!" The musical voice came from below.

Giselle looked down the mountain slope. "Angelica!" she called. "I am so glad you're okay! I was worried. How did you get away?"

Angelica climbed effortlessly up the steep incline and stroked the pony's neck. "They did not even see me," she answered. "But I was only able to mislead them for a short time. They are backtracking toward your trail right now. However, the children still have a few minutes to rest."

"They need all they can get," said Giselle. And so did she. Even the hard cave floor wouldn't keep her awake for long, she knew.

"While they are resting, there is something we must do."

Despite her best efforts, Giselle's shoulders sagged. She wasn't going to get any sleep after all. Stop whining, she reprimanded herself. At least Angelica has a plan. That's more useful than a bit of sleep. She patted Domi on the neck. "Okay," she said. It was hard keeping the exhaustion from her voice. "We might as well get started."

It hadn't taken long to find the trail, the right trail this time. The agent strode ahead, keeping a sharp eye out for the bewitched fibers. There were none to be found, which was good. He was fed up with wasting time, with Claude and his stupidity, with the hot day, and most of all, with the girl and her sly deceptions.

He would keep it simple from here on out – track the children as fast and efficiently as possible, and then haul them back. There would be no more letting the guard lead. No more smoke breaks. No more following false trails. And if the golden filaments appeared again, he'd use the machete to clear their path. There'd be no more stopping for any reason until the children were under his control again. Now was the time for quick, decisive action.

Later he'd think of revenge.

"Inside this cave there is someone who may help us," said Angelica. She walked to the entrance and looked inside.

"The hermit woman?" asked Giselle, though she didn't know for sure the woman actually was a hermit. She just couldn't think of any other reason for someone to live alone on a mountain.

"Yes." Angelica looked surprised but quickly recovered. "We must ask her to show us the way we must go to cross the mountain."

Giselle nodded. "I hope she listens to you better than she did to me," she said. She followed Angelica into the cave. Gray stone walls stretched back into oblivion, and Giselle felt a thrill of fear. "She's back there?" she asked, her voice hushed.

Angelica nodded. "She is. Keep close behind me," she instructed. "We do not know what we will encounter."

"What about Domi?"

"He will follow."

The cool airflow revived Giselle as they walked deeper into the cave. The tick of Domi's hooves against the rocks was comforting as he paced along behind. Giselle stopped once to rub his forelock. He was so calm and tranquil, even in this strange place, and his quietness lent her strength. Not that the cave was that bad – but soon they would be beyond the reach of the light coming from the entrance. If only she had a lantern or a candle.

But oddly, when the cave opening disappeared behind a corner, Giselle could still see. She didn't understand how. There was no source of light, yet everything was subtly illuminated – almost as if light was floating within the particles of air. But that was impossible.

The passage narrowed and twisted, went up and down hills, and they walked on and on. Dark corridors stretched away from their own path and, after a few minutes, Angelica turned down one, then detoured down another. It was a labyrinth.

When the older girl disappeared around a bend in the passage, Giselle hurried to catch up. She rushed around the corner and almost ran into Angelica standing at the edge of a large cavern. Light streamed in through a hole in the ceiling, and a small cooking fire crackled in the center of the chamber, illuminating the man and woman perched beside it. The couple stared at them in confusion and fear.

"We will not hurt you." Angelica said quickly. Her voice was gentle. "Please do not be afraid."

Giselle waited for them to laugh. Of course she and Angelica wouldn't hurt them. How could they? Neither of them were a match for the woman, let alone the man. But the adults didn't laugh. In fact, they seemed frightened. "We need your help," Giselle added, suddenly hopeful.

Her words prodded the woman into action. She leapt to her feet and helped the man stand. Then, taking his hand, she helped him stumble out of the fire's brightest light.

Giselle looked at Angelica. Why wasn't she doing anything to stop them? What if the adults escaped down one of the tunnels dotting the chamber? "Wait," she called to the fleeing couple. "We only want to talk to you." She took a step forward, her hand held out.

"Go away!" the man stopped to yell back to Giselle. "Leave us alone!"

"But I only..." started Giselle, and then stopped. The terror in the man's eyes was disconcerting. Why was he so afraid of her? She was just a girl. She couldn't hurt him if she tried. "But I'm not..." The man limped into the shadows and the woman followed close behind. "...going to hurt you," finished Giselle as the adults disappeared through a dark slit in the rock wall.

She slumped to the ground, defeated. They'd failed. Now what were they going to do? The men were coming. According to Angelica, they'd soon find the children's trail – if they hadn't already.

They were coming closer with every second, and Giselle didn't know where to take the children or how to help them escape. And even worse, the only people they'd met who could help them had just refused. Why? There was no reason. All they needed from the hermits was information. Where to hide. Where to find water. If there was a trail over the mountain. That was all. Yet they'd refused to even listen. Domi nuzzled Giselle's arm, and a sob burst out, breaking the echoing silence of the cave.

Angelica touched her shoulder. "I am sorry, Giselle," she whispered. "But we cannot force them."

Giselle hiccupped. "It's not your fault, Angelica," she gasped, her voice loud in the stillness. "But I don't understand. Why wouldn't they listen to us? No one cares what happens to us. Not a single person." Another sob. Tears sprang from her eyes. "I don't know what to do. I don't know how to save the children."

"I thought they would listen. I am sorry," Angelica repeated, her voice sadder than anything Giselle had ever heard.

"No, I am sorry," said a strange voice. Giselle and Angelica looked up to see the woman standing in the cavern again. She'd come back. "We know what it's like to have no one care," she continued. "We know what it's like to be reviled and cast aside and desperate. I will listen."

"Thank you," Angelica said. "With all my heart, I thank you." She drew a deep breath. "Come, let us sit by your fire for a moment. Come, Giselle. Domi."

Giselle dashed away her tears and hiccupped again.

"Would you like something to drink?" the woman asked.

Giselle nodded, not trusting her voice yet, and walked to the fire. The woman picked up a long knife from beside the blaze and turned to grab a coconut from behind a rock. She swiftly removed the outer layers, then knocked the top off the coconut with one swing and held it out. Giselle took it gratefully. The first liquid mouthful was the best thing she'd ever tasted in her life and the second was even better. She knew she was guzzling the coconut milk, but couldn't stop. Her body was crying out for nutrients, and the rich liquid was like nectar in her mouth. Finally, feeling slightly ashamed, she held the coconut out to Angelica.

"You finish it," said the golden girl. "I am not thirsty."

Giselle needed no more encouragement and a few seconds later the coconut milk was gone. She wiped her mouth and looked at the woman. "Thanks," she said, and hoped her voice portrayed how grateful she was.

The woman nodded and sank to the ground beside the fire. The firelight flashed across her face, heightening the whites of her eyes. "My name is Maura," she said.

Angelica introduced herself and Giselle, and then asked, "What of your companion?" She indicated the dark passageway behind the woman. "Will he not join us?"

"His name is Thierry, and he is my husband. He won't join us yet. He wants me to tell you his story first."

"Why?" Giselle couldn't help but ask. Was there something wrong with him? She remembered how he'd limped when he left the fire.

102

"Because, once you know more about us, you may reject our help," Maura said simply.

Giselle laughed. The statement was so ridiculous. "No way," she said. "You have no idea who's after us. Restavec agents. They're catching up to us right now, and we can't escape without help. We have no food, no water. The littlest kids are totally exhausted, and we don't know where to go. We're beyond desperate."

The woman raised her eyebrows. Then the worst thing she could possibly say came from her mouth. "And in order to escape your agents, Giselle, would you accept the help of a zombie?"

They were making excellent time. The trail was fresh. They were only a short distance behind the restavecs now, the man was sure. The brats were moving slowly. He could see where small feet dragged in the dirt. They must almost be ready to drop with exhaustion.

Not that he was full of energy himself. The sun was directly overhead, burning down on them, sapping their energy. Claude kept falling behind, only catching up when the agent stopped to examine the tracks.

But he wasn't going to stop. He'd made a commitment to keep going until they had the kids back, and even if he had to leave Claude behind, he was sticking to it.

Giselle leapt to her feet. Maura was a zombie? But how could she be? She looked normal. She might be overly thin, but other than that, she looked like an average woman. So it must be the man, Thierry. Her eyes searched the dark crevice. Was he watching them from the darkness, thinking evil thoughts? Laying a vicious trap for them?

"Giselle, sit down," Angelica said gently. "There is nothing to fear here."

"But..."

"Sit down."

"He will not hurt you. I swear," added Maura. "He was a zombie, it is true, but he will not hurt you. We can help you hide from your agents. But first, you must accept us."

Domi nickered behind her, and Giselle's arms encircled his neck. She laid her head against his warm hair and his heartbeat swelled to fill her mind. His heart rate was slow and steady. Domi wasn't afraid. Giselle looked at Angelica. Neither was she.

"Please, Giselle, we must listen," said Angelica. "Remember we are running out of time."

Slowly, hesitantly, Giselle nodded and lowered herself to sit on the ground, this time a little farther from the woman.

Maura sighed and clasped her hands in front of her. "You've probably heard the stories of what zombies are, that they're the dead brought back to life. I thought the same too, for years, but that isn't the truth. They don't die, though their loved ones believe they do. Instead, they're drugged. It's a powerful drug, made from blowfish and other poisonous creatures and plants – and from bones." She paused for a moment and shuddered, despite the warmth of the fire.

"It's made by voodoo priests and anyone can buy it, if they have enough money. In Thierry's case, his brother wanted his land. He must have used his life savings to buy the poisonous powder. He sprinkled it into Thierry's shoes, and when the poison soaked in through his feet, Thierry became sick. He became so sick that he eventually fell into a deep, deep coma that made him appear dead. And that is what we all thought – that Thierry had died. Even the doctor was fooled."

She paused and looked toward the dark crevice. "And worse, I was fooled," she said softly. "I was broken-hearted when Thierry died. It was right after we married. We buried him, or thought we did, and…it was terrible." Emotion choked her voice and silence engulfed the cave.

Giselle gasped as the man limped from the shadows. Her first impulse was to jump up and run away before it was too late, before he had them in his clutches, but something in his dark eyes stopped her – sorrow. Scars crisscrossed his body, and with every step, his leg twisted outward, as if it had fractured and then healed crookedly.

He isn't a monster, Giselle realized. He's just a sad, broken-spirited man.

When he reached his wife, Thierry lowered himself awkwardly to the ground. "My brother put sandbags into the coffin and everyone thought I had been buried," he said, continuing the tale. "But instead I was sold to an evil man who beat me and forced me to work in his sugar plantations far away. I was a slave there for years with many others. None of us were even aware of our situation because the overseers kept putting mind-numbing drugs into our food to keep us docile. So we worked. For years all we did was work. Unaware. Uncaring. I would have been there until I died, like so many before me, if a miracle hadn't happened."

Maura explained. "His leg was broken in an accident, and the plantation owner didn't want him anymore. He threw Thierry off his land, and without the steady dose of drugs, Thierry came back to his right mind. He remembered me. And when he could walk, he came home."

Thierry continued the story. "The problem was that no one wanted me there but Maura. Once a zombie, always a zombie, in their minds. They threatened us. Maura was fired from her job as a schoolteacher. No one would hire me to work. When they burned down our house, we knew we had to leave," he said. "And so we came here. We've lived on the mountain for two years now, suffering cold and hunger, heat and more hunger, just because my neighbors were afraid and superstitious. Just because they were narrow-minded."

Giselle shifted her eyes to look into the fire. Before today, she was one of those people. If she'd been one of Thierry's neighbors, she wouldn't have been mean to him, but she would've desperately wanted him to leave.

But I was wrong. She looked at the man sitting across the fire from her. He wrung his hands together as he stared into the flames. He was abused and trapped, thought Giselle. Being a zombie is kind of like being a restavec, except they're drugged so they have no idea they're really slaves. And they have no hope of rescue because the people who love them think they're dead. How horrible!

"So do you want our help?" Maura asked.

Giselle looked up. All three of her companions were gazing at her, and she could almost feel Domi looking at her from behind, waiting for her answer. "Yes," she said, without another moment's hesitation, and then to emphasize her answer, she repeated, "Yes. Yes, please."

The afternoon was becoming unbearable. The sun blasted them from above, and heat rose shimmering from the earth. The agent didn't know how much longer he could stand it.

The children will probably be resting, he reasoned, half desperate. They wouldn't walk through the hottest part of the day, not when they're so tired. Maybe we can stop for a few minutes. Have a short breather.

He looked up the slope. There were two caves on the bluff above that would be cool, and it would take only minutes to hike up to them. Or even better, they could rest beneath those nearby coconut trees. It would be shady and cool enough beneath the branches, and maybe they could even find a coconut or two. He could use a refreshing drink right about now.

And then, if Claude fell asleep, he'd sneak away for a couple minutes and eat some of the jerky he'd put in his pocket yesterday. There was no point in sharing. After all, he was doing most of the work, and he was the one who'd had the foresight to carry a bit of food with him. Claude didn't deserve any.

Giselle started back the way she and Angelica had come, but Maura stopped her. She shook her head. "No, not that way. Follow me."

"You know where they are?" asked Giselle, surprised.

"I've been watching all of you," Maura said. "There's a passage leading into the cave where they're sleeping. We'll bring them back here, and then Thierry and I will lead you through the caves. Your pursuers won't follow us far. They'll be afraid of being lost in the darkness." She took two burning sticks from Thierry and handed one to Giselle. "So you can see," she explained.

Thierry handed a third stick to Angelica. "Are you not coming with us?" asked the golden-haired girl.

Thierry shook his head. "I can't," he said. "You must hurry and I'll slow you down too much. And there's one place I can't cross."

"What about Domi?" asked Giselle. "Can he cross?"

"No. He can stay here with me."

Giselle looked at Angelica to see her nod to the man. Apparently, she completely trusted Thierry with the pony.

"Let's go," said Maura. She started toward the back of the cave. Angelica was right behind her, but Giselle hesitated beside Domi.

"I'll take good care of him," said Thierry gently. "Don't worry."

Giselle searched his face. There was still no malice there that she could see. No ill will. "Okay," she said and patted Domi one more time. "I'll be back soon, buddy."

Maura paused before entering the crevice. "This is a dangerous cavern, so be careful where you step," she warned, then added as an afterthought, "And don't be startled by the cave spiders."

Great, thought Giselle. Something else out to get us. But the thought didn't make her as afraid as it would have yesterday. She'd already faced worst things than cave spiders and survived.

Without hesitation, she followed the others into the passage.

The man stood and stretched. Their rest had been short, but he already felt rejuvenated. "Let's go," he said gruffly, and kicked Claude in the leg. Then he smiled and kicked again.

"Stop that!" The guard turned over to glare at him. "I'm no dog that you can kick!"

The agent merely grunted and turned away to look in the direction the tracks led. How far away were the children – just a few hundred yards – or a couple of miles? Either way, he was anxious to get going.

He turned back to see the guard straighten to his full height and glare at him with angry eyes. For the first time, the agent wondered if he'd gone too far. He couldn't have Claude quit now. He needed help getting the kids down the mountain. "Here," he said and shoved a half-filled coconut shell toward Claude. "Are you still thirsty? Have a drink."

The guard paused, his eyes locked on his boss's, and then reached to take the peace offering. He drank the rest of the liquid, broke off some of the white meat inside, and popped it into his mouth. He glared at the agent as he chewed.

"Hey, look what I found in my pocket while you were sleeping," the man said to him. He had to do something quick, before Claude decided to walk away. Reluctantly, he pulled out the last of his jerky and held it toward Claude. "You must be hungry."

This time Claude seemed to accept his unspoken apology and grunted, "Thanks," as he reached for the jerky.

"You ready?" asked the man, trying to keep the resentment out of his voice. That jerky was supposed to be his supper. His knuckles turned white as he gripped the machete.

"Yup," said Claude, totally oblivious. "Let's go."

At first, the passageway was easy to walk. The walls were close but the floor was flat and the ceiling high. The interior was dry, and Giselle didn't see any spiders skittering away from her meager light. They walked for a few minutes in relative ease, and she was beginning to wonder what was so dangerous about the passageway, when she saw a dark shape on the floor ahead.

It's a black rock, she thought. But then why doesn't the light shine on it?

"Keep to the far right now," instructed Maura. "The pit is deep."

Giselle gasped. The blackness wasn't a rock. It was an elongated hole covering the floor of the cave – and the only way past was a narrow ledge running along the side.

With precise movements, she followed Maura and Angelica onto the rocky shelf and slid along the cave wall. The ledge narrowed the farther she went, until the abyss was just inches from her toes. And to make matters worse, her torch was going out. Only Angelica's stick seemed to glow with any strength.

For a moment, Giselle thought of throwing her dying torch into the pit, but then she changed her mind. She didn't want to see how deep the pit was. If the torch fell out of sight, she might be too petrified to continue. She shuffled two more steps, and accidentally sent a pebble careening over the edge.

She froze. Seconds passed and there was no sound. She'd almost given up, thinking the pebble must've landed too quietly to hear, when she heard the ping from far below. The pit wasn't bottomless but it might as well be.

If she fell in, she wouldn't be coming out again. Sweat beaded her forehead despite the coolness of the cave.

Her torch tip had faded to mere embers. With one swift motion, she flung it over the edge and pressed back into the rock. At least now she

had two hands to hold on with. But she still had to make her feet move again. Even a few inches would be good.

Giselle shut her eyes, forced herself to imagine a wide path stretching along the chasm, and shuffled along the shelf. More stones rattled over the edge, this time from Angelica or Maura. There was a long, long silence, longer than the last time, Giselle was sure. She didn't realize she was holding her breath until – ping ping ping – the pebbles struck the bottom.

Keep going, Giselle commanded herself. Just one more step. Just one more step. The chant in her brain seemed to work. Just one more step. One more step. One more step. One more. One more. One…

A warm hand touched her shoulder and her eyes sprung open. Maura stood beside her, the light from Angelica's stick illuminating her amused face. Giselle didn't care. She almost collapsed in relief when she saw she was past the chasm. Well past.

"You should go to the children first," said Maura. "They might be frightened if they see a stranger."

"Okay," agreed Giselle, her voice shaking. Maura was right. The woman seemed like a nice person, but after living on the mountain for so long, she looked wild. The last thing they needed to do was send the children scurrying out of the cave. "I'll call you when it's okay to come out," she added with a little more composure.

Angelica gave her torch to Maura and walked with Giselle along the twisting passageway. Together they rounded the final corner to see the children sprawled across the floor with their eyes closed and mouths open, sound asleep. Even Paul, who looked like he might have tried to keep watch, was snoring against a boulder at the cave entrance.

"They're exhausted," Giselle explained, not wanting Angelica to think the children were simply careless.

"Yes, and they showed much fortitude in walking all last night," replied Angelica. "I was impressed with their strength."

"I wish we could let them sleep," Giselle commented as she picked her way through the sleeping bodies.

"Me too." Angelica bent to wake Amelie.

Giselle touched Paul's shoulder. When he didn't stir, she shook him. He opened his eyes, groggily, and then sat up straight. "I didn't mean... I'm sorry... I... but..." he stammered.

"It's okay," said Giselle. "But we have to move on. The restavec agents are on our trail."

"And we must be quiet," added Angelica, joining them at the cave entrance. She gazed down the mountainside. "They are near."

Giselle's eyes searched the vegetation. She couldn't see anything. How did Angelica know the men were there? Before she could ask the question aloud, Angelica spoke again. "Yet it is puzzling. They have passed by the caves and are moving farther from us in that direction." She pointed.

"They're following the false trail I left," whispered Giselle, incredibly relieved she'd thought to waylay the men. "I tried to dead end it on a rock slide."

"Maybe they'll lose the trail," suggested Paul, hopefully.

"Maybe," said Angelica, but she sounded doubtful.

"Let's hurry and wake the children, and then tell them about Maura and Thierry," suggested Giselle. "The sooner we get going, the better."

The trail was easy to follow until they hit the rockslide. When the man couldn't find any tracks on the other side of the jumble of rocks, he sent Claude up the slope and he walked down. He didn't go far before he realized the brats must've gone up. Though they wouldn't leave any tracks on the rocks, their pony, with his hard little hooves, would leave some sign of his passing, no matter how subtle.

Within moments of walking the upper slide, he saw scuffmarks on a stone. He smiled a grim smile. The sign was so obvious, and yet Claude hadn't seen it.

But the agent's smile didn't last long. He was feeling far too vulnerable out in the open. And the mountain was starting to get to him, its big, brooding presence hovering over them, watching them. The quiet seemed tense, not peaceful. The occasional bird shriek was jarring. Every sound sent a zap of alarm down his spine.

His mood didn't improve when after ten minutes the single scuffmark was still all he'd found. He watched Claude search along the top of the slide, and then climb down toward him. The guard shook his head when he reached him. He hadn't found anything either.

The agent shuddered despite the blistering heat on the slide. It was as if the girl, the children, and the pony had all vanished into thin air. Even after everything that happened, was he still underestimating her strange powers?

Finally Giselle, Paul, and Angelica had the children on their feet. Giselle didn't dare let them sit. Tiredness radiated from their eyes, and she knew that if she let them relax, even a bit, some would be asleep again within seconds.

"There's someone I want you to meet," she said when she finally had their attention. "Angelica and I found someone to help us." Quickly she told them of meeting Thierry and Maura and how the adults had promised to lead them through the caves and on through the mountains to the children's village.

"But why would they want to help us?" asked Mark suspiciously. "No adults ever wanted to help us before."

"They're used to being misunderstood themselves," Giselle answered. Then she quickly told the story of how the couple ended up in the mountains. "But he's not a zombie now," she concluded. "You'll see he's okay when you meet him."

The children looked at her with horror-filled eyes.

"Meet him?" asked Tyla in disbelief.

"Thierry will not hurt you. I promise," said Angelica, doing her part to reassure them.

"I don't want to meet him," Amelie said firmly.

"Me either. Zombies are..." Paris couldn't finish her sentence. Apparently, she could find no word terrible enough to describe zombies.

"He isn't a zombie anymore," countered Giselle.

"I don't want his help either," said Paul. "What if he lied to you? What if he's planning to kill us? Its better to be a restavec than dead." There was a murmur of agreement among the children.

"He didn't lie to me," said Giselle. "He's telling the truth. Angelica believes their story too."

"But, Giselle..." Paul glanced at Angelica, and then looked back at

116

Giselle. "She's kind of different too. She seems nice, but maybe she's really in on it with them. Maybe she saved us so she could lure us here."

"Thierry's not lying to me, and neither is Angelica. I swear," said Giselle. She was getting frustrated. How was she going to convince them? Why were they being so stubborn?

"But you might be wrong," stated Mark.

Giselle looked at her little brother, standing with the others. "What about you, Robert? Are you brave enough to go through the caves with Thierry and Maura? I'll be with you too." If only the little boy would say yes, maybe the other children would follow his example. But Robert merely ducked his head and put dirty hands over his eyes.

Giselle knelt in front of him and pulled his hands from his face. "Robert, listen to me. It's okay to be scared. I am too. But you have to trust me." Her eyes moved to the other children, to each face in turn. "You all have to trust me. There's no way we can make it through the caves alone. It's a labyrinth in there. There are openings everywhere, and cave spiders too, and worse, deep pits. Only Maura and Thierry know the way."

"But he's a zombie, Giselle," said Paul, as if that was the final word.

Giselle stood. "Will you at least listen to Maura?" she pleaded. "Maybe if you talk to her, you'll see she wouldn't hurt a fly. And Thierry is just the same."

Paul hesitated and looked around at the others. They were all staring at him, willing to trust his decision. "Okay, we'll listen," he said turning back to Giselle. "Because you believe her, we'll listen."

The agent directed the guard to walk in ever widening circles from the scuffmark on the stone, and he did the same. Individually, they searched every stone, every bit of dirt. The slide was growing hotter by the minute, and heat rose in shimmering waves around them. The sunlight felt like a sledgehammer beating against the agent's brain. He straightened and wiped the sweat from his brow.

This was her fault! She was behind everything that had thwarted him. Not only had she escaped, but she'd tricked Claude and then stolen the children, hidden the cop from them, found a pony for the smallest kids to ride, fooled him with the golden thread, led them astray – and now this! He could almost hear her laughing at him.

His own laugh was like a sudden bark, and Claude looked at him sharply. "She thinks she's got us now," the agent said, feeling lightheaded in the heat. "But she's not going to win. I don't care what tricks she uses. It doesn't matter if she erases their tracks with black magic. We'll get her. We'll get them all back."

Claude mumbled something the man couldn't hear.

"What? What's that you said?"

The guard scuffed at a rock with his boot. "Nothing, Boss."

"Tell me!" Suddenly he felt even hotter.

"It's just, uh, you know. She's just a girl. She ain't no witch or anything. I know you think she's got these powers, but…"

"You think she's just a girl?" the agent screamed, his head instantly filled with the rush of his own heartbeat. "You're an idiot! A stupid, thick-headed moron! You think she's just an ordinary girl? You're beyond stupid! How could she do all the things she's done, if she was just a girl?"

A wave of dizziness washed over him and he slumped to a large rock. "And how'd I ever end up with someone as senseless as you?" he continued to scream. "You're nothing but a big ape! A big, lumbering, brainless ape!"

The guard glared at his boss, his entire body shaking with sudden rage. He silently clenched and unclenched his fists.

Clench. Unclench. Clench.

Then, without another word, Claude stalked off the slide, heading back the direction they'd come.

Giselle hurried toward the back of the cave. "Maura," she called. "You can come out now." When Maura came around the corner, Giselle quickly explained the children's reluctance to trust her and Thierry. "You can convince them," she concluded. "I know you can."

"I'll do my best," said Maura and squeezed Giselle's hand.

When Maura made her appearance, a murmur ran through the group of children. The woman immediately sat on a large stone at the back of the chamber and took a non-aggressive stance. She spoke in a soothing voice as she started to retell the story.

Behind the children, Giselle fidgeted. This was so frustrating! Maura was talking so patiently to them, so leisurely, as if they had all the time in the world. And they didn't. They had to hurry.

What if she'd missed a hoof print at the edge of the slide and the men were walking toward them this very moment? What if they decided to check the caves, thinking the children might be resting there? It made sense for them to do that. The caves were the only cool place nearby to rest on a hot, hot day. The men might even climb up to rest themselves, surprising both the children and themselves. She'd feel much better when they decided to trust Maura and could leave.

But what if they decide to not trust her at all? The thought was unwelcome. What if the children use all our escape time listening to her, and then decide to not accept her help? How do we get away?

We don't, she realized abruptly, and dread swarmed over her. The little ones can't run far enough or fast enough to escape without a head start. Maybe Paul will get away. Maybe even Mark or Kristine. They're the oldest. But the rest will be recaptured.

And the worst thing is, it doesn't have to happen. All they have to do is trust me, trust Maura and follow her into the caves. All they need to do is put aside what they've always believed about zombies.

Suddenly, Giselle didn't feel so confident.

When Claude disappeared into the undergrowth, the agent knew he'd gone too far. Slowly, he climbed to his feet. He wished he hadn't said the words, but it was too late. And he wouldn't go after Claude. His pride wouldn't allow it.

But maybe there was no need. Something had caught his eye. He followed Claude to the edge of the slide. Two coarse, light gray hairs clung to a branch. The pony's hair!

He looked down. There were no tracks. But the pony must have come this way. Could Claude be right? Could she be just an ordinary girl, though a very crafty one? If so, what would a very crafty girl do to hide her tracks? She'd sweep them away. And where would she go then?

His eyes rested on a grove of trees. She'd take the kids into the shade. They'd be as hot as he was out on the slide.

A slight noise sent him spinning around. When he saw nothing there, he looked up at the mountain, the Mont des Enfants Perdus, the Mountain of Lost Children – nicknamed the Zombie Mountain. It was so quiet, brooding, a vast heartless presence staring down at him. And now he was alone!

The man shivered and forced his gaze back to grove. The quicker he found the children, the quicker he could leave this horrible place.

Giselle noticed Angelica beckoning to her and moved silently to the entrance of the cave. Something was wading through the jungle of vegetation down below. She could see flashes of movement though the undergrowth.

"Do you see?" whispered Angelica.

Giselle nodded. "What is it?" she whispered back

"One of the men. They have separated."

"He's going back to town." Giselle's whisper was triumphant.

Angelica nodded. "Yes," she said, but she didn't sound relieved.

Giselle looked at her sharply. "What is it?"

"I would feel much better if the other man gave up too. He must be very committed to your recapture." She looked at Giselle with anxious eyes. "The children must decide soon."

"I know. Maybe we can use this to make them hurry," suggested Giselle and turned back to the group.

The situation didn't look good. Maura had fallen silent and her face and bearing seemed defeated. The children weren't asking questions, and their eyes seemed as suspicious as ever. Paul's stance was still defiant. Paris' face was still frightened. Robert was chewing on his fingernails, something Giselle knew he did only when he was nervous. With a sinking feeling in her heart, she realized that Maura had done her best to convince the children. And they hadn't been convinced.

He was right. There were clear footprints in the dirt beneath the trees. And they all looked the same size – again. Had he fallen for the same trick a second time? Had she led him away while the children were heaven knows where? On the other side of the slide? Halfway up the mountain? How was he going to find them now?

With a roar, the agent sunk the machete's tip into a tree trunk. How could a mere girl have beaten him?

Or had he been right earlier? Was she really much, much more? Had leading him to the zombie mountain been her plan all along?

"Everyone, listen to me," said Giselle. "One of the men is down below. Now don't panic!"

But it was too late. Two of the children screamed. Three more ran toward the back of the cave to stand beside Maura.

"Shhh," said Angelica. She looked down the mountainside. "Oh, no. He has stopped. He heard you."

Giselle felt as if her heart would lurch from her chest. "Is he coming up this way?" Please say no! Please say no! If he comes up here right now, it's over for us. Even if we fight him, someone will get hurt. She glanced at Robert fearfully. She couldn't bear it if something happened to him. Or any of the others.

Angelica kept close to the cave wall and stared down the mountainside. Seconds seemed to drag for minutes, minutes for hours. Finally, she turned to the frozen children. "He turned back the way he came. He must be planning to join again with the other man. They will both be coming."

"Oh no," whispered Giselle. Soon both men would know exactly where the children were hiding. It was only a short walk from the rockslide to the cave. They'd be back in minutes. She turned to the children. "Can you trust Maura? Can you trust me to know what's best for us? Please, you have to decide. Now!"

The agent stopped. What was that noise? Something was crashing through the bush, coming swiftly closer. He jerked the machete from the tree and took a defensive stance. If it were a zombie, he'd have no chance of escape. He'd be killed, or worse, made into a zombie himself. He'd almost prefer a large predator. Then he'd merely be killed.

He couldn't have been more surprised or relieved when Claude burst from the undergrowth. Yet he didn't lower the machete. It was still possible Claude had come back to attack him. The guard had been furious when he'd stomped off. Of course, maybe he regretted his rash decision to leave too. The agent waited for him to speak, waited to decide.

"The kids," gasped Claude. He pointed up toward the hillside, and then bent down and put his hands on his knees. "Around the corner there. I heard them."

"Where around the corner?" asked the agent, lowering the machete.

"In a cave. I'll show you." Claude straightened to look his boss in the eyes. "I need the money from these kids," he said. "That's why I came back. But after this job, I quit."

The man nodded slowly. He didn't want to appear too eager. It wouldn't do to have Claude know how relieved he was to see him. Let the guard think he was taking him back out of kindness. "Show me where they are," he commanded.

The children looked at Giselle with frightened eyes. No one answered her.

Paul turned to face the children. "I think we should try to outrun the men and the zombies," he said. "We can leave right now. Climb up the mountain."

"But the little kids will be caught," Giselle wailed. "Don't you see? The men are faster. Their only chance is through the caves."

"They'd rather be restavecs than zombies," repeated Paul, looking back at Giselle.

"But the stories about zombies aren't true. They're going to be made restavecs for no reason. Please, you all have to believe me." Tears rimmed Giselle's eyes when the three children near Maura edged away from her. "Don't you understand? You're throwing your lives away," she said, holding her hands out to them. They sidled over to stand beside Paul, their choice made. Giselle spun around. "Angelica, can't you do something?"

The girl returned Giselle's look sadly. "No," she said. "We cannot force them."

Giselle turned back to her little brother. "Robert? Do you believe me? You do, don't you?" Her voice was desperate.

When he refused to meet her eyes, Giselle slumped to the floor of the cave, her head in her hands. If Robert didn't believe her, if he couldn't trust her, then what chance did she have with the others? None. They were doomed. Even her. There was no way she'd leave her little brother now. It was over.

The men had won before they'd even caught up to them. Not because they were smarter. Not because the children couldn't escape if they wanted to. No. They'd won simply because the children couldn't – wouldn't – change their prejudices. They'd rather believe the stories about zombies than the truth.

When Claude pointed to the cave entrance, the man felt a momentary thrill of fear. The girl would be in there. Would she have more magical tricks up her sleeve – more ways to sabotage them?

No! He couldn't fall into this trap again. Claude was right. She was just an ordinary girl.

Yet there was one way she'd be different from the others – he'd enjoy breaking her spirit far more. They hadn't hurt his confidence the way she had, hadn't made him appear the fool. In fact, he could hardly wait to get started. Breaking her down, bit by slow bit, would be his reward for all the trouble she'd caused him.

And she was so close. So close!

"They are down below," said Angelica, gazing out the cave opening.

"You can see them? Both of them?" asked Paul, panic replacing the stubbornness in his voice.

"Yes. They will be here in two minutes or less."

There was a sudden hush as everyone in the cave stopped breathing. Giselle watched the struggle in their eyes, saw their fear of the men battle with their long-standing horror of zombies. Then Robert ran to her side. "I believe you, Zellie," he said. "I'll do what you say."

Relief exploded through Giselle's body. Maybe she and Robert had a chance after all. She stood with her little brother in her arms. "Please," she said to the rest of the children. "Come with us. Don't make us leave you here."

A fear far greater than anything Giselle had yet seen appeared in the younger children's eyes. Almost as one, they rushed forward. Giselle felt her eyes tear up with gratitude – but there was no time to waste. "Paul? Mark?" she asked. "What about you?"

"I'm with you," said Mark hurriedly.

Paul was concentrating on the ground.

"Paul? We have to hurry. They'll be here in less than a minute."

He looked up just long enough for Giselle to see it in his expression – acceptance. He'd do what she asked as well. He was either too afraid of the restavec agents or he didn't want to run alone.

"Come on. Let's go." Giselle grabbed Amelie and Robert's hands in hers and hurried them to Maura. The others crowded behind her. When they reached the woman, Giselle bent to look into Robert's eyes. "You go with Maura," she said, and then looked up at the group. "I'll be right behind you, okay?"

Robert nodded and cautiously took the woman's hand. Tyla took her other hand and the others walked behind. Within moments, the huddle was out of sight around the corner.

128

Angelica ran from the cave entrance. "They are here," she whispered. The two girls shrank into the shadows at the head of the passage, and Giselle strained to hear their approach.

Boots scraped on rocks, shadows appeared, and then the men were visible outside the cave entrance. The smaller man walked in front with an eager step, a machete swinging in his hand. The larger man strode behind. Giselle hadn't seen the guard in daylight, and the size of him made her tremble. He looked so strong!

"I thought you said they were here," the boss said. He tapped the machete against his leg.

The guard didn't seem to notice the threatening gesture. "They were here."

"Well, where are they, then?"

It was a logical question, and one Giselle knew wouldn't take them long to find an answer for. There was only one escape other than the main entrance, and they would find it as soon as they walked to the back of the cave. The problem was the children needed time to cross the chasm trail. There were so many of them and they'd be frightened. They wouldn't be racing along the narrow shelf.

And Maura doesn't even have a torch this time! The thought sent another shudder through Giselle's body. The woman was familiar with the chasm trail, but it would still be incredibly dangerous without a light.

"I must go to the children," whispered Angelica beside her. Her voice was almost too quiet to hear. "They need light."

Giselle turned incredulously to Angelica. Had the older girl read her mind? "Where will you find…"

"I will explain later. You must come too," said Angelica insistently.

"In a minute," Giselle whispered back. "You go ahead."

"Do you think that girl's playing another trick on us?" The boss's voice was loud and aggressive.

The big man merely shrugged.

Angelica looked at Giselle. "Are you sure?" When Giselle nodded, she faded back around the corner. "If you need me, call."

When the older girl disappeared into the darkness, Giselle turned her full attention back to the men. Angelica was getting the children light, doing her part. But they needed more than light. They needed time. Giselle knew she'd never forgive herself if one of them stumbled and fell into the chasm because of hurrying. She had to slow their pursuers down – but how?

"There's plenty of sign they were here." The boss was speaking again.

"Maybe they found another way out of the cave," suggested the guard. His eyes swept the shadows where Giselle was concealed.

"That blasted girl…" Anger exuded from the head agent's voice. "She's taken them deeper into the cave. Well, they can't get far without light."

"We'll get her, Boss."

Silently, Giselle moved back along the passage, her thoughts racing. How was she going to delay them? She couldn't confront them. They'd capture her easily, even if she fought with every bit of strength she had. And there was nothing she could do to block the passageway, or hide it.

But there was an idea there somewhere, she was sure. She could feel it. She just needed to think, to somehow calm down and think – with the two men just yards away, one with a machete, the other as big as a horse, both of them walking toward her, and both of them furious. At her!

The man hesitated before stepping into the shadows of the passageway. If the girl was evil, she'd be more powerful in the dark. They'd be easier to catch unaware too. She might send boulders down onto their heads. Or maybe throw some black magic their way and make them irresistible to cave spiders. How he hated spiders! If only he hadn't thrown the matches away.

Claude waited behind him impatiently. After a couple of seconds, the guard cleared his throat.

With every sense screaming No, the agent stepped into the blackness. He couldn't let the guard think he was frightened.

But was being labeled weak worse than walking into a trap set by a witch?

Deep inside the passageway, Giselle looked back. For an instant, she saw the smaller man, the boss, silhouetted against the faint light seeping around the corner. His shoulders were hunched and his movements cautious. She could even hear his erratic breathing. Then his silhouette was engulfed by the form of the big guard coming up behind him.

But Giselle had seen enough. The hunched shoulders, the breathing, it told her one thing. The boss agent was frightened. Of the dark? Or was it more?

"What's taking you so long?" The guard's voice echoed along the passage.

"Shhh. She'll hear you," answered the boss.

Giselle pressed back against the cold stone.

"So? She can't run away. Unless she can see in the dark."

"She might... you know." His voice was hushed.

"She's no witch," the guard said in a mocking tone. It was obvious to Giselle he disliked the head agent, so much in fact, that he didn't seem to care the smaller man was his boss. "I told you, she's just a girl," he added.

There was no reply. But Giselle didn't need to hear a response to understand. The boss was definitely afraid – of her. For some bizarre reason, he thought she had supernatural powers. Thus the hunched shoulders. Thus the cautious movement. And that would be her advantage.

I need to give him reason for his fear. I don't know any spells, but if I make him think I'm evil... I know! I'll make him think I'm trying to trap him. Enslave him. That's something everyone's afraid of. Me. The children. Thierry and Maura. And even though these men don't mind handling restavecs, I bet they don't want to be slaves!

The men were creeping closer. As silently as possible, Giselle moved farther away from them. The chasm was still around a few bends in the passageway and she'd have to stop them before they reached it. She

paused at the first corner and ran her hand along the ground, searching for rocks.

"What's that?" The boss's voice was shaking. "Did you hear that?"

"It's nothing," answered the guard.

Giselle laughed softly, just loud enough for them to hear. She tried to make the laugh sound unafraid, satisfied, even cocky.

"She's here. She's here!"

Giselle took a deep breath and spoke. "No need to be afraid," she said in a thin, sneering voice. "Come forward. Come forward." She tossed a pebble a few yards toward the men so they'd think she was closer than she was.

There was absolutely no sound from the men.

"I've been waiting for you," Giselle added in her disdainful voice and tossed another pebble, this time a little closer to them.

"Get away! Get away from us!" The boss sounded terrified. There was the sound of a scuffle in the dark.

"Calm down," said a deep voice. "She's playing a trick on you." Then silence again. Was the guard holding his boss, stopping him from running away?

Giselle laughed again, her voice deadly soft. "Come forward." She tossed another pebble. "Slaves."

A scream pierced the cold air. The guard yelled. Someone crashed to the cave floor and then there was the sound of scrambling feet. They were running away! Giselle almost cheered aloud.

A split second later, she was glad she hadn't. As the sound of the fleeing man vanished down the passageway, there was closer, subtler sound, a boot scraping against stone. One of the men was still there.

Giselle swallowed nervously. "So you alone shall serve me," she said, packing her voice with contempt.

"Save your breath," the man snapped. "You're not fooling me." Then he stomped in Giselle's direction, honing in on her voice.

The agent didn't stop until he was outside the cave. His legs shook like jelly and cold sweat studded his brow. He'd never known such terror! Almost against his will, he sagged to the ground.

So he'd been right all along about the girl. She was a witch. Or a zombie queen! If he'd been wrong about anything, it was that he'd underestimated her. He looked back into the shadowy cave. There was no sign of Claude. The guard was probably a goner. But it was his own fault. He deserved whatever fate he got.

The man lurched to his feet and staggered down the mountainside. He'd lost the machete somewhere in the darkness and had no way to protect himself now. He had to get off the mountain by nightfall.

And then what? With no children, and little money left, what was he going to do?

He shuddered. It didn't matter. He'd escaped, and that was all that counted. There was only one thing he knew his future would not hold. He was never going to be a child labor agent again. It was too dangerous if you happened to get the wrong child.

135

Thank goodness I caught Maura and the children before they reached the chasm. There is only one way to get the children safely and quickly across.

But it will weaken me terribly. What if Giselle needs me and I cannot go to her? She is back in the darkness, bravely facing the men alone.

Who do I help, Giselle or the children?

The children. I will help the children, for that is what Giselle would wish.

Come, my little ones. Come to the edge. Do not be frightened. I will not let you fall.

Giselle faded back around yet another corner. She had one advantage over the guard. Neither of them could see, but she'd been here before. She'd seen this passage in the glow of Angelica's torch and could remember a lot about it – like the stalactite that hung from the ceiling near the third turn in the passage and the sudden rise in the floor just beyond. It gave her the advantage of traveling faster, quieter, and, as long as she was careful, without injury.

They were about halfway to the chasm now. She tried acting like an evil witch a couple more times, but the guard merely laughed at her. Desperately, she searched for another plan. There were only three more twists in the passage before she reached the chasm. Only three more corners to round, and then what? If the children were still there, she'd have to make a stand, however useless. And if they were across, there was only one thing she could think to do – huddle in the dark and wait for the big man to tumble into the chasm. But the idea made her feel sick. She didn't want to kill him, just make him give up.

Suddenly, she stopped short. A faint light shone around the corner ahead of her. It could only mean one thing. Angelica was still lighting the children's way across the chasm trail. Giselle had come too early.

But I had no choice. He's been pushing me so fast.

And now she'd have to move even faster. She had to be out of sight before he came up behind her or he'd see her silhouette against the light. At least she could see well enough to run.

She slowed when she rounded the bend. Only one more twist in the passage and she'd be at the chasm. The light was much brighter here. How could Angelica have created such a strong torch, so bright that it shone around two corners in the cave passageway? It seemed impossible.

"What's this?"

The voice was well behind her, but Giselle froze anyway.

"Another one of your tricks?"

137

"Do not make me wait any longer for you, Slave," Giselle said in her spooky voice, just in case the man could still be frightened. The light might even help. But she didn't wait to hear a response. She had to get to the chasm. The light was much too bright. Something very strange was happening, she was sure.

She rounded the last corner and stopped short. Of all the crazy things she could've imagined, this was not one of them. Sparkling light stretched from one end of the chasm to the other and the children were walking across it.

It was a bridge – a bridge made of light!

My energy is gone. Domi, you are here beside me. Your tears are beginning to fall, beginning to restore me. I am so grateful for you, my love.

But I can feel your unease. What is wrong? Your girl needs you too? Yes, go to her. Bring her across the bridge. You have given me enough strength to keep the bridge powerful for another minute. You should have plenty of time to bring her across.

Go now. I will be fine.

"Zellie," Robert's voice came from the other side of the chasm. "Come across. It's hard like glass."

Giselle put her fingers to her lips and pointed back the way she'd come, to let them know the guard was behind her. Then she motioned for them to go ahead. Maura understood. She nodded to Giselle, and then shepherded the children out of sight along the passage.

Giselle walked to the edge of the chasm and touched the glowing filaments. They tingled against her toes. She pushed her foot two or three inches into the light before she felt resistance. The bridge wasn't hard as Robert had indicated. Either he was exaggerating or the bridge had grown weaker since he'd walked it.

Okay, I just have to cross, just one step at a time. Yet still she hesitated, looking over beside the chasm. The narrow shelf looked much safer than the magical bridge.

But I can't do that, Giselle realized. The guard will see me and will know how to get across too. And he'll know I'm not evil or magical if I can't even walk on a magical bridge. No, I have to walk on the light.

Ripples of luminance lapped against her toes, and Giselle looked up to see Domi walking across the bridge toward her.

Thank goodness, she didn't have to do this alone! Domi was coming to meet her.

Taking her courage in hand, she stepped out onto the light. She sank almost to her ankles before hitting a firm surface. She took another step. The wispy light clung to her feet like a bright fog. Another step. No problem.

Suddenly she noticed she could see through the bridge. The light brightened the jagged, deadly rocks spearing up from the pit far below. If she fell…

Domi nickered to her and she tore her gaze from the pit. Keeping her eyes locked on his, she took another step. Don't look down! Another step. Another. Another. And then she was at Domi's side, halfway across the bridge.

"Thank you, buddy," she said when she reached the pony's side. "Thank you for coming to get me. I don't think I could've done it alone."

The pony nickered again and Giselle leapt to his back. But when Domi tried to turn back the way he'd come, Giselle stopped him. An unwanted realization had come to her. She could use the light bridge to finally get rid of the guard. There was no need for him to fall into the pit or to continue on to recapture the children. With the light bridge, she could finally convince him she was someone to fear.

"Trust me, buddy," she whispered to the pony. "We'll go soon, okay?" She reached down and took some of the light clinging to her feet and smeared two lines across each cheek, then leaned forward to rub the rest into Domi's forelock. Then with the sly smile of a zombie queen on her face, she waited.

Domi snorted and Giselle felt him fidget beneath her. A tremor ran through him. Giselle allowed her eyes to drop.

What she saw almost took her breath away. Domi's legs were slowly sinking into the light. And the light filaments were fading! How long would the bridge last? Did she have time to scare the guard?

A movement caught her eye. It was he, uneasily advancing around the corner. His mouth hung open as he stared at the light bridge, at Domi, at Giselle. Then his gaze darted to the side, to the trail beside the chasm, and Giselle knew she had no choice. There would be no running for her.

"I have been waiting for you," she hissed. "What took you so long?"

The man's mouth snapped shut and he appraised her with wary eyes. She could almost see him running different possibilities through his mind.

"Come closer, Slave." she beckoned to him. And he stepped closer!

No, don't do that! Just be scared! Just run away! But her voice was calm when she spoke. "That is good. Now come closer still."

She slid from Domi's back and whispered into his ear. "Go back, buddy. This won't take long. And you're sinking too fast." She pushed his head around and patted him on the shoulder. To her relief, the pony turned, however reluctantly.

The guard was almost to the edge of the chasm now. "My horse servant will tell the others to expect us soon," Giselle said, hoping she didn't sound too silly.

"I don't know how you did this, but I don't think…" He paused for a moment. "You're just a girl."

Giselle felt she was going to die with fear. How could he not be terrified of her? Or maybe he was scared, just not enough. Was that it? She could see the alarm in his eyes. It may not take much to push him that little bit farther. But how? "You are right. I am a girl. An ageless, timeless girl." To Giselle's relief, her voice didn't echo her fear.

But the man wasn't convinced. He stepped onto the light bridge – and sank halfway to his knees. Giselle could feel herself sinking too. The bridge was going to give way soon. Very soon.

Hold his eyes. Hold. She sank deeper. Don't look away. Smile a knowing smile. Don't think of falling. Hold his gaze. Hold it. Hold… "I am the Zombie Queen! See my kingdom, below!"

The guard looked down through the light bridge. Instant terror flashed into his eyes and he cried out, spun around, and lurched for the edge of the pit. With panicky movements, he scrambled up onto the solid rock.

"I will give you one last chance!" Giselle yelled in a shrill voice. She stretched out her hand. "Your place waits for you below!"

The guard stood frozen on the edge, seemingly unable to move. Milliseconds passed like hours.

Decide what you're going to do! She was thigh deep now. Decide! Any second, she was going to break through. But until he was out of sight, she couldn't run. She couldn't do anything, except slowly sink through the weakening filaments – then fall to the jagged rocks below.

Giselle opened her mouth to scream – and at the last moment, shaped the primitive wail into words. "Never steal my children again! They are mine! Only mine!"

And the big man ran. Halfway to the corner, he stumbled and sprawled across the rocks. His eyes were glazed with terror when he looked back. He staggered to his feet and limped around the corner. His boots scraped against rocks as he ran farther down the passageway.

Giselle couldn't feel anything against her feet anymore. Instead, she felt she was floating in a fog. She used both her hands and feet to turn, as if she was swimming.

And the light let her go.

Domi, thank you for returning. Thank you for healing me. I must act. Now!

Giselle fell with no coherent thought, only terror. Fear was the blood that coursed through her veins. Horror shrieked through every corner of her mind. She was going to die! She couldn't bear the thought of seeing the jagged rocks rush up to meet her, so she shut her eyes and waited for her life to end.

Something tingled against her leg and her eyes popped open. Was she dead? Was it that easy? But no, a cord of light encircled her ankle. And she was no longer falling. She was suspended in mid air, a wicked looking spike just a half yard below her.

The cord of light lengthened to wrap around her body, as soft as silk, as gentle as a warm breeze. Then it tipped her upright and lifted her out of the chasm.

Angelica stood at the brink of the pit with Domi at her side, the light cord attached to her hand. With her eyes closed and her brow wrinkled in concentration, Angelica reeled Giselle closer, closer, and then set her down gently a yard from the edge. Giselle sagged to the ground when the light released her, her legs too weak to take her weight, and Angelica slumped down beside her.

"Thanks," Giselle gasped.

"You are welcome," whispered Angelica, and she smiled a wan smile. Then the cord of light fizzled to nothing, leaving them in the dark once again.

"It was you all along, wasn't it? You were the one they were afraid of?" asked Giselle. "Somehow they knew you were magic?"

"They never saw me," explained Angelica. "When I played my tricks on them, they assumed I was you. I am sorry. I should have warned you."

Giselle took a deep breath. "No, don't be sorry," she said. "It turned out for the best. I'm just glad it's finally over."

"Me too." Angelica's voice was even weaker.

Domi's hooves struck stone as he moved closer in the darkness. Slowly, Giselle stood and reached for him. She touched his hindquarters, and then stepped cautiously toward his head. "I'll help you get on Domi," she said to the older girl. "You sound tired."

"All I need is a minute to rest," Angelica answered her.

Giselle reached to stroke the pony's face, and pulled her hand away, puzzled. His face was wet. "What's wrong, buddy?" she asked, suddenly worried again.

"He is fine," said Angelica, sounding stronger.

"Do you think he has dust in his eyes?" She could hear Angelica stand beside her.

"No, he is fine. I cannot explain now, Giselle, but he has given me a gift in his tears," said Angelica.

"His tears? What gift?"

"I will explain another time. Here, Giselle. I have something you will need. Take this."

Giselle gasped when soft light swelled around them. She took the glowing white stone from Angelica's hand. "It's beautiful," she said, turning it this way and that.

"So you and Domi will find your way in the dark," said Angelica.

"Aren't you coming with us?" Giselle looked up sharply.

Angelica shook her head. "I will see you again on your trek through the mountains. But for now, I must go. Another needs me."

"What? Who needs you?"

But Angelica just smiled. "That I must explain another time as well. Now hurry. The children are waiting for you in the chamber where we first met Maura and Thierry. I will come again soon."

Caramel, my princess, give me a minute or two to regain my strength.
Then we shall search for your lost daughter. Do not worry. She is alive.
The people who stole her from you have not harmed her.
However, it will take much effort to free her.
And now, I am ready. Come, let us begin the chase.

It took the children, Domi, Maura, and Thierry four days to walk
through the mountains. They traversed the caves, crossed creeks and
tramped through forests, clambered up hills and down into wild valleys.
They ate coconuts and other wild foods along the way, as well as Maura
and Thierry's dried goat meat, and they drank from mountain streams.

Giselle tried not to worry about Angelica, but it was hard, especially the
fourth day when they hiked out of the mountains and started walking the
dry, dirt roads. Despite what she'd said, Angelica hadn't appeared once
during their long walk. It was as if she'd vanished off the face of the
earth. The thought of her out there all alone bothered Giselle, no matter
how many times she told herself that Angelica could take care of herself.
What if she was hurt or starving? What if she was in trouble and needed
help? Giselle longed to turn back to look for her, but her duty lay with the
children. When they were safe, she would go back for Angelica.

Mid morning, they interrupted a friendly-looking farmer working in a
field beside the road. To Giselle's great relief, when they asked directions,
he didn't act like he'd never heard of a Children's Village. Instead, he
pointed farther down the road, told them to turn right at a crossroads and
to look for a walled compound with a red gate on the left. The houses and
school were inside the walls, he said, the fields and gardens outside. He
only looked at them strangely when some of the children cheered.

Giselle knew she'd never forget her first glimpse of the Children's
Village. They turned a corner and there it was: a pure white jewel glistening in the late afternoon sun. A girl in a clean, sky-blue dress was leaning
against one of the gateposts, reading a book. She looked up and shaded
her eyes against the sun to see them better, and then ran to alert the others.

By the time Giselle's bedraggled group arrived at the red gate, an entire
crowd had gathered. A businesslike woman came forward to meet them.
"Who are you?" she asked curiously, after greeting them.

"We're orphans, Madam, running from child labor agents," said Giselle. "We escaped and came across the mountains. Tell me please, is this the Children's Village?"

"It is. And you are welcome here."

Seven simple words. Giselle thought they were the most beautiful words she'd ever heard. Tears sprang from her eyes. Their journey was over. They'd found a home at last.

The children were given a hot meal, and then the headmistress sat them down and started to ask questions. There was so much to tell, yet Giselle could barely stay awake to tell it. The last few days had been exhausting and now, with a full meal in her stomach, all she wanted to do was sleep.

Finally, the headmistress smiled and said they would talk more the next day. Giselle fell fast asleep almost as soon as her head hit the pillow, happy in the thought that Maura and Thierry were staying at the Children's Village too. Maura had even been offered a job. As luck would have it, the Children's Village was looking for another teacher. The headmistress had even offered Thierry steady employment, teaching carpentry skills to the older children. When Thierry insisted on telling her of his past, she said she wasn't a superstitious woman and that was that. There was no more mention of zombies.

Giselle dreamed that night of a scarlet-haired girl racing across the prairie on the back of a fire-red mare, a yearling filly galloping behind. A silver moon hung above them, and grass bowed beneath their flashing hooves as they galloped on and on. She could feel their exultation in the run, in the burn of their muscles, in the wind through their manes – and their joy in being reunited.

Finally, the dream horses stopped on a hilltop and the girl slipped from the mare's back. Her hair shimmered gold as she caressed the mare's neck, stroked the filly's forehead – and disappeared in a flash of light.

"Giselle!"

Giselle sat up in bed. Had someone called her? She looked across the room. Robert was fast asleep on his bed. She smiled. It was nice seeing her brother in a bed. He'd never had one before.

She was glad her dreams had awakened her. This could be her chance to find Angelica, with Domi's help. She slid from beneath her covers.

The moon hung like a silver pendant in the star-studded sky. Giselle found it hard to believe that just a few nights ago she'd been running through the streets of her old town, trying to escape the restavec agents. She'd changed so much since then, and so had the other children. They were all more confident and hopeful, and much closer to each other – almost like a family. Maura and Thierry were even acting like parents toward them. Everything had turned out wonderfully, more than she could've even imagined, thanks to the people from the Children's Village and Angelica. If it was the last thing she did, she was going to make sure Angelica was okay.

"Domi?" whispered Giselle when she came to the darkness of the stable. Everything had worked out miraculously for Domi too. The headmistress had promised to send Madame Celeste money for the pony. He would belong to all of them now.

"Giselle." The voice flowed from the darkness like the softest melody.

"Angelica?"

"Yes, it is I."

Giselle heard rustling in the straw, a nicker from Domi's new stable mate, Tia, and then Angelica walked into the moonlight with the gray pony behind her. "Oh, Angelica, I am so glad you're okay! When did you get here?"

"Just now. I stopped to say goodbye to Domi first." The moon glistened across her golden hair.

"Goodbye?"

"Yes, I will not see you again, Giselle, unless Domi or you need me." She beckoned to the younger girl, and together they walked toward the gate. It was locked for the night. The compound was peaceful and quiet.

"What do you mean?" asked Giselle.

"I have a gift for you." Angelica stopped and looked at her with amber eyes. Her hair suddenly swirled in a nonexistent wind, and Giselle watched her capture a single strand, twine it around a slender finger, and tug sharply. She clasped the hair between her hands and dropped the hair into Giselle's outstretched palm.

But it was no longer a hair. It was a necklace, as gold-colored as Angelica's locks and as light as air. A strange energy tingled to warm Giselle's palm. Gently, she touched the necklace with her finger.

"I've never seen anything so beautiful," choked Giselle. "You can't give me this. It's too valuable."

"Its value is beyond that of mere money, Giselle," said Angelica. "It is the link between us. If you ever need help, touch it and call my name. I will hear you and I will come."

"You will? You'll come to help me?" Giselle said breathlessly.

"Yes, as fast as I can," answered Angelica. "I am sorry to be abrupt, Giselle, but I must tell you this quickly. I may be called away, and there is one more thing you should know. Maura and Thierry owe you their lives."

"But..."

Angelica held up her hand to hush her. "You needed them to go through the caves, it is true. But they needed you to bring them here. You saved more than the children and Domi, Giselle. You saved Maura and Thierry too. I thought you should know. Now you can see that sometimes our actions have unintended results, even wonderful results, when we do what we believe to be right."

Giselle didn't know what to say. She had saved Maura and Thierry? Could it be true? But even if it was, she hadn't done it alone. Angelica had been there to help her. Giselle threw her arms around the older girl. "Thank you, Angelica," said Giselle. "For everything."

Angelica pulled her close for a moment, her arms strong and tingling with energy. "And I thank you," she whispered. Suddenly, she stiffened and released Giselle. "I am sorry, but I must go. Vivo is calling me!" She stepped away.

"Vivo? Who is Vivo? What's wrong?" But even as she asked, Giselle knew it was another question she'd never get an answer to.

"He is trapped. Frightened..." Angelica's voice faded as her body brightened. Suddenly, she erupted into brilliant light. Her golden hair billowed around her head like a luminous halo. And still she grew brighter. Brighter.

Giselle put her hands over her eyes. Angelica was too bright. She wondered how Domi could stand to look at her, but then, his eyes must be closed too.

When the light streaming between her fingers disappeared, Giselle lowered her hands and opened her eyes. Angelica was gone. Domi nickered and nuzzled her shoulder, and she threw her arms around his neck. "What an amazing magical being she is, Domi," Giselle said in a mane-muffled voice. "And strange. And wonderful."

She inhaled his sweet horsey scent, then slowly released him. Together they turned to meander back to the stable. "And best of all," continued Giselle, stroking his neck and looking up at the night sky. "Best of all, she's our friend."

152

Vivo. I am here. I am sorry, my friend. I cannot pull you from this mud hole. I know you are frightened. I know you need help. But you must be brave. The one destined to rescue you will be along shortly.

Yes, the one coming is human. I know you are terrified of humans, my dear one, but you must be strong. Your future is tied to hers. And even more, the survival of your herd depends on her, and her alone.

Be brave, my love, be strong. I will stay with you until she comes.